THE

LEPRECHAUNS

OF

DORCHA WOOD

by

A Isobel Sutcliffe

Illustrated by Maxine I Sutcliffe

Table of Contents

ACKNOWLEDGEMENT

Dedicated to my family. A special thank you to my daughter, Maxine, without her patience and skill this book would be only words. To my friend, Gail Jewel, for your valuable critique. To Randall Andrews, my editor and writing coach, thank you for your patience and inspiration. To the beautiful people of Writers World, you inspire, educate, and amuse me.

Map of Dorcha Wood

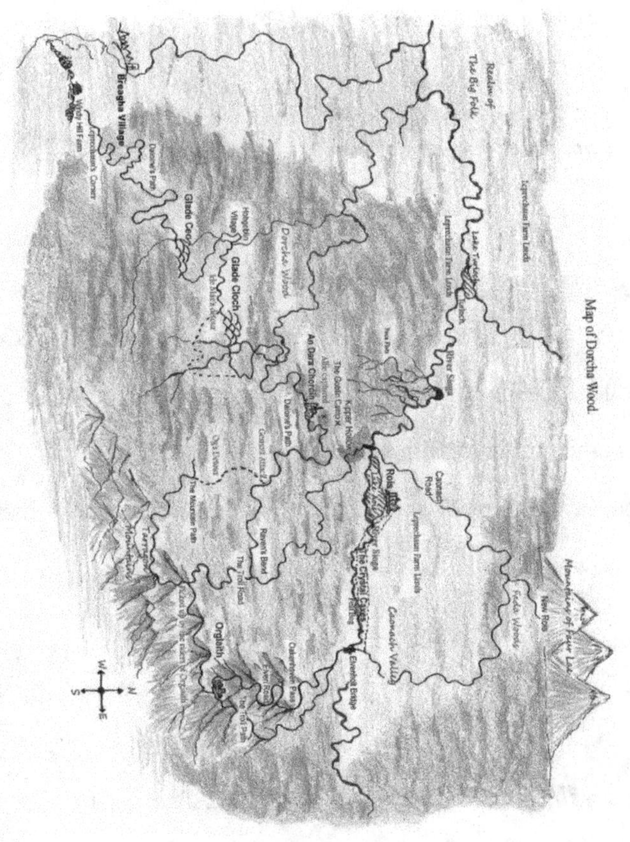

Oh curst toad of legend tell,

of a prince whose worthy kingdom fell·

Only a kiss from a fair princess,

has the power to break the sorcerer's spell

A cry on the wind rent the darkness over the tilled earth, a lament for dreams unfulfilled—of regret and sorrow for past wrongs and transgressions, of angry intent and longed for revenge, of grievance for dearth and hindrance at those hands whose power prevailed—a long keening wail.

****

Ah begorrah! What a racket—whining and shrieking! Keep it down, for pity's sake—the children are sleeping!

Greetings young ones, I am Taliesin the Bard, the teller of tales and singer of songs:

Heed the tale of what befell me in the spring of 1588 when one of my more odious works offended The Encantar and she curst me to speak in limericks for eternity. It happened in the city of An Dara Choróin, in the heart of Dorcha Wood. She demanded the king's allegiance and when he refused, she cast a hideous curse upon him. Inspired, I composed a ballad, not my finest I confess and it fell on peevish ears, but in my defence, I'd had a restless night with Clurichauns running around, yelling and disturbing my slumber. I was beholden to that big dark haired man who arrived wielding his sword. He challenged the witch and... Eh? You ask what are Clurichauns? Well this tale is about Clurichauns, and other wee folk. It takes place around a century after that fateful day, but where to begin. Oh, I know—the start is a fine place to begin, so take a seat by the fire and hearken.

Once upon a time, long ago in old Ireland, there lived a tiny maiden. Fair of face, her hair was scarlet and every strand upon her pretty head had a gilded tip...

1

<u>The cry on the wind</u>

Allie O'Hara slipped out of bed mousey quiet and climbed onto the chair. She inched opened the wooden shutter and the cold, damp air swirled on her face. She paused and took scarcely a breath as she listened through the darkness for the sound that disturbed her dream—the dream that trickled away and out of memory. A cricket chirruped but she daren't clap her hands to hush it. Her younger sister Ciara slept in the bed beside hers, the sound of steady breathing told the noise hadn't invaded her sister's dreamless sleep. Minutes ticked by and Allie turned from the shutter.

You were dreaming.

As she climbed down to the floor, it came again. Away in the distance a high-pitched scream and a tinkle of musical laughter. Allie froze.

Is that the sound I heard?

She couldn't be sure. She didn't remember hearing laughter the first time. She tried to recall what she'd heard; a long wailing sound—or was it?

What in the name of Ériu did I hear? What could make such a sound—a banshee?

A single leap put her back into her bed; a single tug, she pulled the cover over her head. As she listened to the thudding in her breast, she cursed her chicken-heartedness. Her mother had taught her ladies had little need of bravery; there would always be a gallant man to assist should she find herself in danger. Allie felt sure, in the life of every girl, the time must come when she'd have no choice but fend for herself.

2

<u>Allie O'Hara</u>

Sixteen and tiny, when Allie O'Hara stood by her father the top of her head reached his hip. Her big, bright blue eyes twinkled when she smiled and her pointed ears poked out through her spikey hair. She ran fast for her size and sailed over the kitchen table as she ran from her brothers. When her tinkling laughter rang through the house, it brought a smile to all, but her mother who scolded her boldness.

"Allie, you're a young lady. Quieten your voice and keep your feet modestly on the floor."

"But Mother, Rían is chasing me…"

"You shouldn't encourage him by playing boy's games. He's a boy, you're not!"

Allie sang, danced and played the little fife Uncle James made from a reed. She mimicked the birds in the apple trees and at times disappeared from view—how, she never knew. Allie never asked why she was smaller than her sister and brothers. She wondered—but had never asked. The children of Breagha Village weren't as kind as her family; they considered her an oddity. They laughed and called her a Leprechaun.

"I'm not! Leprechauns have curls, my hair is straight!" Allie wasn't sure about this; she'd never seen a Leprechaun.

"It's red like a Leprechaun."

"But it has yellow tips, so there!"

"Why doesn't it grow? You've never had a haircut but it's always short."

Allie didn't know why her hair was so. She longed for hair like her younger sister. Long and dark, soft and feminine. Hers was short, spiky, and red as the poppies that grew in the summer; each strand had a golden tip. In her community, girls her age were already women full-grown; several planned their weddings. Allie didn't think any man would want a wife the size of a five year old. She didn't want to marry anyway, though she worried about her place in the community. She knew the family who loved and cared for her was not her birth family, that much her adoptive parents had revealed but she loved them as dearly as they loved her. They never mentioned her size and Allie assumed herself small for her age.

Mary, her adoptive mother was small and dark haired, she knew her letters, uncommon for a woman in old Ireland. She sewed her family's clothes, spun and wove the wool of the sheep they farmed into warm rugs she sold at market along with the excess food they grew. Life was hard, but the O'Haras were a happy family, respected in County Breagha. Mary taught the letters to all her children, Kean, Rían, Allie, and Ciara, telling them knowledge was freedom.

Allie's adoptive father Patrick had many stories. Tales of the wee folk, unicorns, dragons, and all manner of strange creatures said to roam the nearby woods—Brave folk who fought wars against evil, of the big folk and little fighting side by side in days of old. Allie's favourite was a chilling story about a bold knight called Máedóc who saved the wee folk from a terrible witch. Her big brother Kean said father told such stories to stop his children from straying too far into the dark damp forest that bordered their farm, the 'Dorcha Wood' forest. Allie didn't mind that her family never had money for they lived in a warm little house and they always had enough to eat. They spent each evening by the fire. Her father told the best tales, some the children had heard many times but were eager for the retelling.

3

The Wee Red-Haired Man

Late afternoon, Allie and her brothers, Kean and Rían gathered firewood and berries at the edge of Dorcha Wood. Golden rays of sunlight slanted against the gnarled trunks that formed a rough arch over the path into the dark woods. The strange sound she heard that morning had faded in Allie's mind for distractions on Windy Hill Farm abounded. Kean, now a grown man of twenty years wielded his axe some distance away, cutting fallen branches at the edge of the woods. Rían gathered sticks and piled them on the old wooden cart. Allie's basket filled to full of the sweet black brambleberries she'd picked from the tangled hedgerow. As she picked the last berry above her head, a piercing scream from a nearby hazel thicket frightened her so; she fell backwards, berries rolled and bounced into the grass.

"Do ye have be makin' such a din, ya witless mule?" A little, belligerent man in a green hat backed out of the thicket dragging a wee black horse by the halter. "Ye scared the Princess wit' ya racket!"

The man, advanced in years but vigorous, stood a tad taller than Allie; he had bright red hair, pointed ears, and big blue eyes. His rough-spun green tunic reached his knees and his breeches tucked into his boots. Over the tunic, he wore a shirt of copper maille; the leather breastplate bore a silver crest with a pink, gem-encrusted rose at the centre. The leather satchel slung across his shoulder made soft tapping and jingling sounds.

He snatched off his hat and bowed deeply.

"Your Royal Highness, at long last! Truly humbled I am, to be meeting yerrself on t'is fine evening!"

The tiny black horse stood on his hind legs and peered at her over the man's shoulder; he continued his spiel, "I have travelled many a long hard mile wit' honour, to bear ye tidings from ye grandsire, His Majesty Finnán Etain, King of Rois". He finished with a satisfied smile.

A blanket of silence covered Windy Hill Farm for a long trifling. Allie sprawled in the grass, surrounded by berries. A cool breeze on her tongue warned her, her mouth hung open and she snapped it shut. Her brothers ran from the edge of the wood and skidded to a halt beside her, Kean brandished his axe at the little red haired man.

"Get back!" He puffed as he shook his axe.

"Good sir an' fellow man-at-arms," the man squawked, "I come in friendship a-seekin' to bear our good King's word to the young princess." He held his hands high and made no effort to draw his hatchet. The little horse drowned his last word with another scream, and earned him a smack between the eyes from his flustered master.

"Princess?" Allie found her voice at last. "King? What King? A—and why are you calling me Princess? You—you must be—you are mistaken!"

"Are ye nary the Leprechaun Princess, Alastríona Síofra of Rois?" The man's face turned pink.

"No! My name is Allie."

"Shush, Allie." Her brother leaned and patted her shoulder. "You'd better come with us," Kean had a tremble in his voice and his face had grown pale. "You must talk to my father. Come Allie, Father will explain."

Allie stared up at Kean, intrigued by his change of manner. Rían too eyed his older brother, but only for a moment. Rían, a growing lad and perpetually hungry, loathed wasting a morsel of food; he gathered handfuls of the spilled berries and dropped them back into the basket. His bundle of sticks and the cart stood in the fading light at the edge of the woods.

The little horse reared on his hind legs, peered into the hedgerow and all around.

****

Windy Hill Farm had belonged to the O'Haras for many generations. The O'Haras were an old family and they, like others in County Breagha, had little wealth, but they lived a mostly comfortable, if not luxurious life. Patrick O'Hara's brother, James owned the farm across the lane; the families lent each other a helping hand. The tiny market village of Breagha lay a short distance along the lane. It had been some years since Leprechauns had come to this end of Dorcha Wood. In ancient lore, the farms of old Ireland all had Leprechauns living nearby. Tales of the riches and protection these wee folk bestowed upon their chosen family, over centuries had become legend.

4

Getting Acquainted

"I'm sorry, I haven't introduced myself," Kean gazed down at the Leprechaun. "I'm Kean, my brother Rían, and as you already know, this is Allie."

The Leprechaun gave a cheery bow and hastened to keep up with the long strides of Kean and Rían.

Allie rode on the cart.

"Tighearnan, son of Tighearnan of Turloug," he declared. "But you may call me Tiggy."

The tiny horse chuckled.

"An' t'is undersized mule, is Og." Tiggy waved a fist in his companion's face and the little creature squealed.

"I've never seen such a wee horse." Rían joined Allie, gazing at the man and his companion. "Where ever did you find him?"

The little animal stood on his hind legs, scanned his surrounds, and trotted to catch up. Og was much smaller than a horse—at his withers he stood half as tall as Allie. Shaped like a horse but with longer legs, he had a thin face with large dark eyes—his mane and tail thick, soft, and silky.

"Oh Og's no horse, he's a Grant. They are mostly useful at watching for danger though Og 'ere screams at almost everyt'ing he sees."

"I heard him scream before first light this morning." Allie remembered the sound to which she had awoken.

"Oh that." Tiggy snorted. "Ye were hearing that? My manservant likes to amuse hisself by scaring Og first t'ing every morning, says it makes him walk faster for the rest of the day." Tiggy cast a nervous glance at the edge of Dorcha Wood.

"Manservant?"

"Uillian, son of Uillian of Turloug. We call Him Willy. He's waiting at camp, back in the woods for my return and I hope he is keeping my supper warm."

Kean took the shaft of the cart from Rían and whispered something Allie couldn't hear.

"But you must have supper with us; we'd be honoured to have your company at our table. Og too." Kean eyed the Grant.

Rían sprinted up the hill towards the house.

****

Hiding in the trees at the edge of Dorcha Wood, a black cloaked and hooded figure leaned on a staff and watched with interest. Unable to leave the forest and enter the realm of the big folk, the figure could only observe from a distance. The sun sank below the horizon and the figure melted into darkness.

When labour, skills and tools abound,

the wee folk will till the ground,

the plants will grow and wise men know,

that toiling drudge with gold be crowned·

We will return to Allie and her companions further along. Now we must journey back in time to a generation, just a stone's throw away to Leprechaun's Corner of Windy Hill Farm. Smoke billowed from the chimney of the wee house that would stand abandoned in Allie's time. The rooster crowed and hens clucked; the chip-chip of the farmers hoe mingled with the birdsong.

5

<u>Leprechaun's Corner</u> (A generation before)

Farmer Torin Etain was a wise man, and a Leprechaun, fiery haired with big blue eyes. Like all Leprechauns, he loved to grow crops and flowers or create things from clay, metal and wood. For many years, he tilled the land in Leprechaun's

20

corner of Windy Hill Farm. He was on good terms with all in the county, Leprechauns and big people alike. Torin was of royal blood, though he never mentioned it and never sought the glory such a title might bring. He found contentment farming his land and raising his daughter, Idé Mae since her mother passed on when the girl was five years old. He looked forward to the times when his cousin's son, Prince Alastor Finnán Etain would come to visit. Torin loved the intelligent and exuberant boy who befriended Farmer O'Hara's sons Patrick and James. Alastor and Idé Mae spent many hours playing with the O'Hara boys in neighbouring Dorcha Wood and around Windy Hill Farm, their shouts and laughter brought a smile to Torin's face. As Alastor grew, he became involved in the daily life of his father's kingdom, and at age twelve, his regular visits stopped.

The years rolled by and Idé Mae grew into a young woman. As she grew, she asked her father about his royal blood.

Torin smiled. "I would have been king but Grandfather Angus the Erratic was a tyrant and was deposed by his brother,

Prince Treasach the Truthful, who took the crown. So my line became ordinary folk for which I am forever thankful."

"Does that mean that I would have been the Queen? I am your only child."

"Yes." Torin tapped out his pipe on a post and refilled it with fresh leaf. He gazed across the tilled land—his day's work. The cool afternoon wind ruffled his hair—more silver than red. "Yes you would, but you're a beautiful young lady who is free to be whatever she wishes. Young Brogan down the road would marry you tomorrow if you'd say yes." He smiled. "Freedom is a rare thing in this world, we here in County Breagha and those in Dorcha Wood should never forget this blessing which has become our birthright. Nary envy young Alastor his crown for he will bear the concerns of protecting his subjects for all his days. Nay, I would not have his burden for all the gold in Rois."

Idé Mae ignored the remark about Brogan and pressed on. "But if it fell to you by, say—th—the death of the King or—or Alastor, wouldn't you take the crown?"

"If there was no other way, but perish the notion. Young Alastor is married now, and I believe his new bride is with child." Torin smiled at the thought. "Nay my child, don't envy Alastor his title."

But Idé Mae did envy Alastor. Envied and resented his title and life. One morning her yearning turned to a burning need. She must take her rightful place as the Queen of Dorcha

Wood and beyond. She imagined the people in the forest paying homage. Dreams of gifts—royal ceremony, of feasts, jewels, riches, and mainly the crown, which she imagined would be made of gold and precious stones.

****

Not far from Leprechaun's Corner, in the shadows of Dorcha Wood, a dark hooded figure at last had cause for hope.

All things in Dorcha Wood have push and pull as on that fateful day when the witch curst me. Nary did she heed her father's words and Idé Mae set off into the woods, her heart's yearning would bring untold sorrow...

6

Idé Mae's quest

A year later, Torin passed on and Idé Mae lingered long enough to see her father buried. She freed her father's livestock and set off before the O'Haras could arrive with kind offerings.

Down Daione's Path into Dorcha Wood without a plan, but Idé Mae knew her desire and would persevere until she wore the crown. To avoid an encounter with the inquisitive

Faeries, she detoured off the path away from the grass and fern covered Mounds of Glade Cloch. She fought through the ancient trees, ferns, and boulders for hours until she became lost. There she made her first and most loyal ally. An enormous Natterjack toad called Fie Fíu. As she rested by a small stream, his huge head popped out of the ferns.

"Hello, my beauty, what brings you this far off Daione's Path?" He wiped his mouth with the back of his warty hand.

Idé Mae flinched. "I–I was avoiding the Faeries of Glade Cloch, they ask too many questions."

"Hmm, and why don't you want to answer their questions, my beauty?"

"My reasons are my own." Idé Mae folded her arms.

"I can sense that you are on a quest." His bulging eyes narrowed. "Yes. A quest." He wet his hands with his big pink tongue and wiped them over his eyes.

Idé Mae wrinkled her nose. "Well, I'll be off," she squeaked.

"Don't be in such a rush my beauty, yes!" The great toad hopped across the little stream and plopped in front of her.

"Tell me about yourself, my beauty, for I like you. Yes, I do like you!"

"Well—" Idé Mae backed away, "I—I'm a princess!" she stammered and hoped this piece of information, however false, would see him mind his manners.

The toad rubbed his eyes again and made a squelching noise. "Princess? Nay, my beauty, I think nay. But you want to be! Yes, oh yes, you want to be!"

Idé Mae sighed. "Yes, I want to be. Not just a princess but a queen."

For the first time, she told her story. He was a large, ugly toad, but she told him of the title she believed she was born to, of the injustice that Prince Alastor would take her birthright, the crown of Rois.

"I mean to have it! I am the rightful heir to the throne."

The toad's eyes fixed on a buzzing fly, his long tongue sprang from his mouth and the fly vanished.

"Yes, you are!" he gulped and wiped his mouth. "Let me help you. Together we'll hatch a plan."

"You? Help me?"

Should I listen or flee?

Fie Fíu's big wet tongue flicked across his lips. He regarded Idé Mae with shrewd bulging eyes.

Idé Mae remained.

Storm the palace! burn the town!

The flags of Rois be cast aground!

The river's mud will flow with blood!

Arise! A new Queen and take the crown!

At this point in our tale, I must make known some of the many creatures herein. The Clurichauns are little folk, the dark side of Leprechauns—trust me, I know. They're not as handsome as we Leprechauns, nor are they as clever. They're not the worst creatures Idé Mae recruited, however. Púcas are dark, furry human-like creatures that resemble a goat—until they change into something else… But let us press with our story, speaking of Púcas gives me the colley-wobbles!

7

<u>The Conquest of Rois</u>

Idé Mae and Fie Fíu became close allies. Over the months that followed, they gathered a secret army of disenchanted

Clurichauns and Púcas, led by a Clurichaun, Ultan the Evil from the village of An Dara Choróin. Fie Fíu knew all the miscreants of Dorcha Wood and brought them together with a promise of riches and power. The army marched on Rois in the middle of a moonless night. Poised to swoop when the fighting subsided, Idé Mae and Fie Fíu followed in a chariot drawn by six black March Hares.

The city of Rois had been at peace for generations, few guards manned the walls and the invasion proved easy. Many Leprechauns died. The remaining population fled without a fight. Ultan the Evil and his most trusted warriors entered the palace, followed at a safe distance by Idé Mae and Fie Fíu. A group of palace guards surrounded the King and moved him north to the safety of the Mountains of Fuar Lae.

****

Prince Alastor and a small assembly of guards fought to defend his wife and infant daughter. He drove back the gang that entered his chamber but when he emerged to give chase, he found Idé Mae in the throne room; she reclined in the King's chair with his crown upon her head and a toad-like smile on her face. She had the Royal Cittern a carved wooden instrument with golden strings clutched in her greedy hands, along with the key to the treasury.

"Idé Mae? How did you get here? What are you doing?"

"Well, dear Prince, as you can see I have crowned myself Queen of Rois, the rightful Queen, after all it was my line that held the crown for many centuries. I banish you, and your family from Rois and indeed all of Dorcha Wood. Go now! Or my Queen's Guard will have your heads!"

31

Alastor sprang and seized the cittern and the key. As he wrested it from Idé Mae, her minions heard her shrieks and squawks; they charged at Alastor with swords and axes. Wounded and bleeding he retreated, the palace echoed to the sounds of clashing metal, of shouts and cries of pain and triumph as they fought for their lives. Flannen, his captain of the guard turned and pushed Alastor back into his bedchamber.

"Quickly, Prince! Take Lilé and the baby and go, we'll hold them off."

Alastor stuffed the treasury key into a carved wooden box with the rest of the palace keys and slipped it into his satchel along with the cittern. He gathered the baby, Princess Alastríona, and beckoned to Lilé. They slipped out a side door and made their way to the river. With the enemy in pursuit, they ran as fast as their legs would carry them and jumped into a boat moored at the wharf. Alastor handed the baby to Lilé and grabbed the oars. As he paddled with all his strength, he heard Lilé cry out.

"What is it?" He daren't stop.

"I'm fine! An arrow has hit me, keep going! I'll be fine."

When Alastor reached the opposite bank, his wife still clutched the infant princess.

"Leave me" she breathed, "I will only slow you down, take Alastríona and keep her safe."

Alastor ignored the pain of his wounds, gathered up his wife and baby and with the powered imbued in him by the blood of his Faerie grandmother—a power he'd never before summoned, flew high into the air over Dorcha Wood, to the safest place his panicking mind could conjure; Glade Cloch. His arrival before dawn, with a group of anxious Ee-shees— the minute guardians of the woods in pursuit, brought the sleep befuddled Faeries from their Mounds. He laid his wife on the grass at the feet of their leader, King Eaghan.

"Please! Help her! She is gravely wounded."

The tiny Guardians of the Woods, the Ee-shees landed around him squeaking and chattering but the Faeries waved them away.

Alas! Neither Faerie medicine nor magic could help Lilé; she had died in her husband's arms as they flew over Dorcha Wood.

"You must give us the baby, you cannot feed her yourself." The elderly King held out his arms for the infant, Alastríona. The new Viceroy stood behind him nodding support. "It is the only way; we will raise her here as a Faerie child and she will be safe. She has Faerie blood."

Alastor clutched the baby to him. "No! No, I'm taking her out of Dorcha Wood; she will be the only remaining heir to Rois and nowhere in Dorcha Wood will be safe for her. Rois has fallen to my cousin Idé Mae and the Clurichauns."

"This is not in the best interest of the young Princess." The Viceroy spoke. "She must stay with the Fae, you too, Prince Alastor, until you are healed. You'll both be protected."

"No! I daren't leave her here, there is a place I can take her where I know she will be safe."

Amid the Faeries, angry voices muttered of treachery, broken trust and alliance with Rois—betrayal of blood connections and indignity at the doubt he cast upon their defences.

A young Faerie moved to Alastor's side.

"We have no right to take the Princess from Alastor!" he called to the angry mob. "I have a child of my own as many of you here have; you know he must do what is right for the safety of his child and himself! We, the Fae must not interfere regardless of blood connections!"

The mob charged brandishing fists and bows.

The Faerie scooped Alastor into his arms and flew into the early morning sky, chased by others of his kind. He flew high and faded against the sky, lost to the eyes of his pursuers. The Ee-shee trailed, they clung to the Faerie but he ignored their squeaking inquiries.

"Where is it you wish to go?" He asked Alastor.

"Take me to the edge of the woods, please, to

Leprechaun's Corner of Windy Hill Farm. The O'Hara's have a child of an age with my daughter; they will care for her."

In the pink of dawn, the Faerie set Alastor down at the edge of Dorcha Wood. He shooed away the Ee-shee as if they were flies.

"You are wounded. Let me see, I may be able to help."

"I'll be fine." Alastor smiled at the Faerie, "Thank you, but what is your name?"

"I am Maghnus, we met once as small children. Are you sure you can make it to Windy Hill Farm? Your wounds are grave."

"Prince Maghnus, of course, I should have recognised you. Thank you, Maghnus, my family won't forget your kindness. Please ensure my wife is buried somewhere close to Glade Cloch so our daughter can visit her grave when she is grown. I know your people and mine will forever be allies."

****

The two went their separate ways; Maghnus back to Glade Cloch to face his angry kinfolk, and Alastor—to his old friend

Patrick O'Hara, to a safe home for his daughter and at last to succumb to the wound from which flowed his life's blood.

A flight to freedom and death to end,

a promise to give between old friends·

With words of love, tears and blood,

a hope for grief the years to mend·

8

<u>A Reunion, a Farewell and a Promise</u>

Patrick O'Hara dug potatoes with his little boy, Kean. It had been a good summer and the cart laden. There would be at least three more trips to the barn before days end and tomorrow they would dig the turnips.

"Plenty of turnips this year to make Jack-o-lanterns for the wee ones," Patrick's smile faded as he gazed towards Leprechaun's Corner, deserted.

Where did you go to, Idé Mae?

The shovel slipped from Patrick's hands as a Leprechaun stumbled into view, his bright red hair fell across a blood-smeared cheek and swollen eye; his green cloak torn and bloodied. He carried a bundle wrapped in a shawl. Patrick recognised Alastor, his boyhood friend whom he hadn't seen for years.

"Patrick! Old friend, t'is shameful only tragedy could bring me here today!"

"Alastor!" Patrick ran to him "What has happened?"

Grey faced and sweating, Alastor fell to his knees and kissed the cooing bundle.

"Ériu bless you wee one." He whispered and held the baby out with shaking hands. "My daughter, Princess Alastríona Síofra of the Rois People. Please! I beg you—protect her! My people will be forever in your debt."

Patrick took the Leprechaun baby and cradled her with one arm. Her tiny fists waved at his face and she gurgled sweetly. Her father collapsed.

Patrick knelt by his childhood friend and took his hand in his. "I'll protect both of you. You're going to be fine I promise." He handed the baby to Kean who stood close. "Hold her." He slipped an arm under the Leprechaun's shoulders.

"No—no, it's over for me. I can go no further, dear friend."

Patrick shut his eyes to the terrible chest wound and a tear rolled down his cheek. The Leprechaun's breathing shallowed as he spoke and fought to hold his eyes open.

"My beautiful Lilé, the mother of my child is dead." Tears of grief and pain flowed, both men wept. "My people are scattered, taking shelter in the Mountains of Fuar Lae. My father is there too—I hope. My cousin, Idé Mae, and the Clurichauns have taken our city."

"Idé Mae?" Blood drained from Patrick's face.

Alastor reached into the leather bag by his side.

"Please, when my Allie is old enough she must have these. Tell her who she is, when she is old enough."

He pulled out an ornate wooden box and passed it to Patrick. His hand moved to take a second item from the bag but fell lifeless to the ground.

9

A Kingdom Divided

Maghnus returned to Glade Cloch to find the Royal Court and the centre of the city in deranged uproar, hostility such as he'd never before seen among the Fae. To his dismay, the fighting broke out between his supporters and those who supported the stance of the king, regarding custody of the infant Princess Alastríona. He'd had differences of opinion with his father, King Eaghan and his advisers. These disputes had escalated when the King elevated Ivor to viceroy. Maghnus hadn't known Ivor until he emerged as an outstanding young Faerie employed in the royal court. His impeccable manners and knowledge of royal procedure had gained him notice by the higher ranks closest to the king. Maghnus had taken a dislike to Ivor, his love of tradition and snobbery, especially when it came to dealing with others in Dorcha Wood, had brought animosity down on Glade Cloch. Ivor the Conniver, the spinner in the shadows; Maghnus could see he had duped the elderly monarch into heeding his council to the exclusion of his older and more experienced advisors. Now his people were in the midst of a brawl erstwhile unseen in the Faerie city, one Faerie had died and many more wounded.

When he arrived at the King's mound, Maghnus reassured himself of the safety of his wife, Ríona and their son. He found them secured in their bedchamber with his sister Princess Madeléine. Reassured, he went in search of the King. When he entered the throne room with two of his own aides, he found old chamberlain Martok, one of the king's longest serving and much loved members of staff, dead on the floor. A young servant kneeled beside him with a dagger in his hand. Ivor, flanked by his cohorts, entered through the door behind Maghnus.

"Murder!" he screamed. "You will pay for this treachery." Ivor's zealous eyes shone, his chest heaved. "Imprison them!"

Into the dungeon prison of Glade Cloch they marched Maghnus, his aides, and the young servant, but despite Ivor the Conniver's best efforts, they released Maghnus and his aides without charge. The young servant protested his innocence, testified he'd walked in and found Martok dead on the floor with the dagger beside him. Nevertheless, they convicted him for the old Chamberlain's murder.

Following the trial the King became ill and confined to bed, Ivor refused entry to all—including Maghnus and Madeléine.

"The King is ill and the healers are with him, he is weak and must not be disturbed until he has recovered. The King is sure you'll understand."

Early the next morning, Maghnus woke to pounding on his door. Ivor and his assistants triumphantly brandished a royal decree to banish Maghnus from Glade Cloch as well as those loyal to him, citing charges of creating unrest in the city. They blamed him for the riot.

Heartbroken, Maghnus left Glade Cloch. He left his gravely ill wife, Ríona, and their son in the care of his sister, Madeléine. Maghnus set out to a place no man would take a sick woman and small child.

"You should stay and fight." Madeléine protested.

However, for Maghnus, who had seen for himself his father's signature and royal seal on the decree, there could be no doubt it was the King's wish. He left Glade Cloch and never intended to return. To stay would mean more bloodshed. His love for his people compelled him to surrender his title.

****

King Eaghan died a week later, and Madeléine assumed the throne in the absence of her older brother. Her first act as Queen was to dismiss Ivor the Conniver and order him to leave Glade Cloch, forthwith. An army of Faeries escorted him from the city, his anger terrible to behold; he screamed curses and threats. Madeléine, her heart broken by the sudden death of her father sought to bring her brother home. His refusal infuriated her. After the burial of their father, Madeléine and Maghnus quarrelled; Maghnus told her he thought it would be in the best interest of the Fae if he remained exiled.

"I want to see change in the culture of the Fae and there are too many here who will fight to the death to keep things as they are. I will not be the cause of more heartbreak among my people. I have already begun building a new Faerie community. As soon as it is established, I will move my family to my new home. I'm certain the people of Glade Cloch would prefer you as their leader."

Many at Glade Cloch did not want him to return, they blamed his dissent for the sadness that befell their city. Madeléine watched her brother leave; both of them grief stricken and bewildered.

****

Ultan the Evil ordered the Clurichauns to throw the dead of Rois in the River Síoga, lashing any who protested. In the cold and sober light of day, the Clurichauns deplored the evil they had perpetrated the night before. Their fear of Ultan, the Púcas, and the giant toad Fie Fíu, saw them carrying the bodies of their Leprechaun cousins to the river, the

47

Clurichaun's tears flowed as they laid them in the water to float downstream. Ultan the Evil carried a cat-o-nine tails, which he used to flay without remorse. When they completed this grisly task, Ultan ordered the Púcas to ensure none of the Clurichauns left Rois.

"Shut the gates, man the parapets." His harsh voice reverberated inside the city walls. "No one leaves and no one enters unless I say so. Is that clear?"

Satisfied with his morning's work, he reported to Idé Mae, perched regally in the King's chair. She and Fie Fíu had been served breakfast by the terrified Leprechaun servants whom she'd spared; a Queen must have servants and Clurichauns made lousy servants.

"Ah Ultan, take breakfast with us," the Queen gulped frog like on a fried egg, for she'd taken on some of the toad-like mannerisms of Fie Fíu. "Then I would like you to break open the royal treasury—since that thief, my cousin Alastor, has stolen the key. My family has much gold and precious stones which I shall need to count."

Hours later, Ultan listened to Idé Mae's voice echoing through the halls of the palace, squawking in frustration, the king's crown perched askew on her head. Her hair in disarray, her throat and eyes bulged alarmingly. They had exhausted all the options and still the treasury remained unscathed—its cool white marble untouched by his hammers and hefty wooden rams. A cannon, with iron cannonballs had failed to scratch the shining surface of the smooth stone.

Fie Fíu slept, evident by the croaking snores that resonated from his gaping mouth, his enormous belly extended skyward; it rose and fell with his breathing. Sprawled out by the window on a resplendent red divan, he had his skinny leg hooked over the crest-rail.

****

High on the palace parapets, a black cloaked and hooded figure, staff in hand watched, gratified. The head nodded once and the figure vanished.

49

We return now to Windy Hill Farm sixteen years after those terrible events. Remember? Allie and the O'Haras have a dinner guest...

10

The O'Hara's tale

Supper proved a subdued affair that night compared to the usual cheery gathering. Tiggy sat on the higher chair normally occupied by Allie who sat on a pile of crates. Og ate a bowl of turnips and greens on the floor beside the hearth. Tiggy scolded him when once more he resumed standing on his hind legs trying to see out the windows. The grant then curled up on the rug and fell asleep.

Allie had exhausted herself crying when she had heard why the O'Haras raised her. Patrick confessed he'd withheld her identity, selfishly hoping the Leprechauns would never come to take her back and that she'd stay forever with them as their much loved daughter and sibling. Mary and Ciara were also puffy eyed and spoke as though inflicted with a bad head cold. Tiggy's arrival had caused heartache in the household as he told how the aging Leprechaun King Finnán wanted his grand-daughter at his side.

"His magic wanes in the mountains of Fuar Lae and he requests the presence of Princess Alastríona. He believes her magic is the Rois people's last hope for she is The Custodian."

"The Custodian? Of what? I have no magic! There must be a mistake; I cannot be the princess you seek. Perhaps you've come to the wrong house."

"Your father, Prince Alastor, told me your full name and title when he entrusted you to my care." Patrick shook his head. "There is no mistake. I don't know anything about what you're custodian of but you do so have magic, otherwise how could you run as fast as your big brothers? How could you jump so high? I've seen you fade and disappear into a wall or a clump of grass many times. What else could that be but magic?"

"Fade?" Tiggy frowned. "What is t'is magic? I've nary known a Leprechaun to fade an' disappear. 'Tis Faerie magic."

"She blends into whatever she is standing near. If you know where she is you can still see her, but it's a good way for her to hide."

The Leprechaun shook his head. "'T'is never Leprechaun magic I know of. Members of the royal family are known to have more magic than commoners, but the ability to disappear?" He looked them in turn, bewilderment etched on his face.

"Prince Alastor had the same ability." Patrick smiled. "I learned never to take my eyes off him when we played hide and seek."

Dinner over, Mary and Ciara cleared the table and brought more berry wine, plates of fresh bramble berries and the soft white cheese Mary made from sheep's milk. The little Leprechaun became expansive with tales of the battle with the

Clurichauns; how there had rose a leader, Ultan the Evil of An Dara Choróin, Idé Mae's Captain of the guard and Mayor of Rois. He had goaded the normally lazy and mostly drunken Clurichauns into attacking the hard working and peaceful Leprechauns of Rois.

"They attacked in the middle of the night wit' the help of the Púcas. Many of the Rois Leprechauns died, many more escaped, most headed for the Mountains of Fuar Lae, along the Caonach Road. They have established a new village in the mountains, but mountainous terrain is nary farmland our people are accustomed to working. The routes have had to change and we can't reach many of those we used to trade with. We suffer for the loss of trading partners and I'm sure they too are suffering. Our people wish to return to the city of Rois but the Clurichauns have it heavily fortified. T'is well guarded day and night and the Rois people are no warriors. They say there is someone who advises the false Queen and has power over the Púcas. Of t'is person I have no knowledge other than to know he exists."

The Leprechaun stared into his cup; lines of worry crisscrossed his face. "I'm unsure what the King expects from ye Princess. He turned his big blue eyes to Allie. "But he is certain bringing ye back to your people will restore them to Rois. And yerrself being Custodian, we cannot act wit' out ye." He put his cup down and sighed. "We'll have to find a way to get back into the city first. I am having ideas on how, but none of them is so good. Ye Grandfather thinks that once the people know The Custodian has returned they'll rally together wit' new hope."

Tiggy and Og took their leave of the O'Haras and returned to the camp in the forest. He said he would wait as long as it took Allie to prepare for the journey.

Allie stared into the fire, tears once again in her eyes. The rest of the family gathered around her.

"I'm afraid," she whispered. "I know nothing of Leprechauns—and worse, I don't know how to fight the Clurichauns or Idé Mae. What am I custodian of? She gazed at the faces of the people she loved, who until a few hours ago she thought were the only family she'd ever know. "What am I to do? How do I know I can trust Tiggy? I can't do this by myself and by the sound of it, if I don't find a way, who will? Those poor people of Rois will be forever doomed. I don't want to leave them to their fate. I wish I knew what to do. I wish I knew how to do it. I wish I had the courage to do what I know is right. The only thing I'm certain of is I am not brave. Even the rooster scares me."

"You won't be alone." Kean's words buoyed Allie's spirits. "You won't be alone because I'll be with you. All the way and I'll be your courage."

"As will I." Rían leaned in.

"No! Rían you have to stay here to help father with the farm," Kean shook his head. "Please, you must! Besides you're a much better farmer than I." He raised a hand to stem his brother's protest. "I'm sure I will be more than a match for a few Clurichauns. What are Clurichauns father?"

Allie looked up, she too wanted to know.

"They are another race of Leprechauns—they usually have brown hair and green eyes. They spend most of their time browsing the woods for any kind of berries they can find, all of which I'm led to understand is made into wine." Patrick sat with his elbows on his knees, his hands hung relaxed and he stared into the fire. "Some say they are the dark side of the wee folk. I don't think that is the case. I'm sure they are the same people, just different in their ways and appearance."

"Tell me all you know about the Leprechauns, Father," Though Allie still struggled with the revelations of that day, she found herself curious about the people who saw her as their last hope.

Patrick frowned and paused. "There are ancient legends, I know not from where they came."

He inhaled and blew it out slowly. "I can only tell you what I know, and tell you what is true and what is legend. The legend as my grandmother told me is this: The Leprechauns came from a race of forest spirits, which served a king in the Dark Ages. He summoned them to his side to guard his gold and treasure. They were fierce warriors whose ferocity was renown throughout Ireland. When the king's reign ended at his death they ascended to heaven by his side— after a time they returned as Leprechauns, descending to earth to live among the big people once more."

A log of red-hot coals broke and fell in the fire with a soft clatter. Nobody moved and Patrick continued.

"That is the legend. What is true is this: There was a whole community of wee folk that lived at the edge of the forest, they farmed part of Windy Hill Farm for centuries as well as other farms bordering Dorcha Wood. Allie, Torin who farmed Leprechaun's Corner of our land was, I believe, your grandfather's cousin. This is how your father came to spend so much time there. Idé Mae is Torin's daughter, though as children when we played together, I never would have believed what she would become." Patrick ran his fingers through his hair, sighed and resumed.

"The wee folk are masters with tools; their skill with wood and metal is legendary. They are also skilled in the art of pottery. The big folk of County Breagha accepted their presence; they treated them with respect and kindness. Many formed lifetime friendships, something not common in other counties. Big and wee folk lived, worked and traded side by side without conflict. They say because of the big folk's kindness, the Leprechauns blessed our county and freed it from overlords—they made everyone equal and happy. The freedom we have in County Breagha isn't a freedom known to all in Ireland. It saddened us when the Leprechauns left County Breagha after the fall of Rois. I keep and maintain fallow the corner of Windy Hill Farm which wee Torin tilled, it is my dearest wish that someday the Leprechauns will return. Indeed, I think it will be the downfall of the county if they do not return soon as the protection they afforded us may fade. Another reason, Allie," Patrick smiled down at her, "why it is important you go to your grandfather, it isn't only the Rois people who are depending on you, but all the folk throughout these lands. We are depending on you."

"Father," Kean's brow creased, "What are Púcas?"

"That I'm afraid I cannot tell you Kean, for I have no idea." Father rose and stretched. "Well, it has been a long day and you have a journey to prepare for on the morrow. Best we go to bed."

Put your life in an old rucksack,

a brand new dream lies along the track·

Put aside the child, an adventure beguiled,

Away to the forest green and black·

11

<u>Preparations</u>

Allie rose early the following morning; she had another question to ask Patrick. She found him with Kean examining an old hunting bow. She jumped up on the wall of the barnyard.

"Father, where is my father—I mean—Prince Alastor buried?"

Patrick looked up in surprise. "I didn't tell you that last night did I? I carried his body into the forest with an idea that I'd bury him near Torin, but the Faeries accosted me. They demanded I take him to the Mounds, and I agreed. It fit that we lay him to rest with his wife. It took me a whole day's march to reach their mounds. Daione's Path twists and turns back and forth through the woods, if I could have flown like the Faeries, it wouldn't have been far at all. They were in the middle of a civil dispute when I arrived at Glade Cloch. I got the impression it had something to do with Alastor, and what had happened at Rois; I didn't wait around to find out. His body is there in a tomb alongside your mothers. I treasure a hope one day we could move them both to Rois."

"Faeries?"

How many other creatures are there in Dorcha Wood?

"Yes, Faeries. No doubt, you'll encounter them on your way; their mound city is on the path you will be following. You must take much care when dealing with them." He looked from her to Kean, "They may try to trick you with their clever words. Also, never thank them for anything; they'll assume you mean to forget the debt and that will anger them. They like to have you in their debt, but who knows? With a bit of Irish luck and Leprechaun charm, you may win them over." He smiled; Allie hoped his optimism was well founded.

"As my parent's bodies are entombed there I assume I am already in their debt. Are they dangerous?"

"Probably capable of it." Patrick shrugged. "But they have ever been on good terms with your people which should be to your advantage. Try hard to keep that alliance. There are much more dangerous creatures in the woods than Faeries I believe, you'll need to keep a lookout. That wee Grant of Tiggy's will be of good service there."

Patrick hesitated a moment, deep in thought.

"Allie, and you Kean, there's something else about the Faeries you should know." He rubbed his chin with the back of his fingers and mused, his face worried. "When the Faeries made me take Alastor's body to the Mounds they demanded I hand his daughter over as well. They seemed to think you belonged with them until you were of age. I refused, I told them Alastor had entrusted you to me. They weren't happy and I'm afraid I left on rather bad terms, so when you encounter them and you will, be as courteous as you can. You

Kean, should take extra care, they may mistake you for me. It's been said that you and I bear a strong resemblance."

Allie and Kean spent most of the day preparing for the journey. Mary, with the help of her daughters, sewed new clothes for Kean and Allie including woollen cloaks to ward off the cold of the coming winter. She went to the village and returned several hours later with a pair of sturdy wool lined boots for each of them.

"Mother!" Kean exclaimed, "These must have cost a fortune!"

"I'll owe Cobbler McIver for several seasons," she smiled, "but I couldn't bear the thought of my dear children out in the wilds in the middle of winter with cold feet." Kean hugged his mother.

Kean and Rían had spent the morning making arrows, fletching them with feathers from the hens wandering the farmyard. The hens were now a few feathers short for the coming winter but Patrick promised he'd make it up to them by sealing the walls of the hen house against the cold wind. Straight, sharp arrows filled Kean's quiver.

The big leather pack they filled with supplies—flour, biscuits, hard cheese, dried berries and apples.

"I wonder will I need to hunt for game?" Kean drew his bow and loosed an arrow at a tree. "I'll take my axe for cutting fire wood. I may need it to chop off the heads of a few Púcas too. That is if Púcas have heads."

Patrick too, had gone to the village with Mary and returned with an Allie sized war hammer. The midday meal over, Patrick produced an old leather bag not unlike the one Tiggy carried and handed it to Allie.

"Your father asked me to give you these when you were older. I've been keeping them safe."

Allie's heart beat fast as she took the bag.

"Well, open it." Rían craned his neck. He and Ciara also saw the bag for the first time for father had stored it in a trunk. Allie's fingers traced the bag made from sturdy leather with silver buckles and stitched by a fine craftsman.

She opened the bag and took out a wooden box. Exquisitely carved, it had a silver badge with the pink jewel encrusted rose, the same as the one on Tiggy's breastplate. She tried to open it but could find nowhere that appeared to have a catch, or even hinges. She turned it over and could hear objects inside, rattling, tinkling and tapping. "It won't open. What do you suppose is in it?"

"Perhaps it will open when you most need." Ciara's face lit up, she loved the tales Patrick told of magic and enchantment. "Like the magical boxes in the stories father tells." Ciara was two years younger than Allie though much taller. Pretty with dark hair and grey eyes like Kean's, Allie would miss Ciara more than any in the family, she'd miss their late night chats—laughing in the darkness until Mary would call out for them to 'Be quiet and go to sleep!'

"There's something else in here." Allie laid the box on the table and reached back in to the bag. She drew out a small cittern—a stringed instrument, its polished wood glowed. The headstock had the same, jewelled rose inlaid. Its strings, five sets of two, were golden. Allie ran a finger over the strings and everyone in the room sat still. The clear ringing tone filled the room, and another sound, somewhere between trilling fifes and bowed strings swirled around the notes.

Allie checked in the bag for anything more and thought it a pity it held no instructions.

Later in the afternoon, Allie perched on the farmyard wall and once again tried her hand at playing the cittern. She found she had a natural ability with the instrument and loved to play, she admitted to herself, its sweet tones helped her sound proficient. The instrument must also be magic she decided, when the hens and sheep fell asleep as she played.

12

The journey begins

In the morning, they woke early and Mary cooked them a hearty breakfast. Packs full, their blankets and warm black cloaks they rolled in leather to keep them dry should it rain. They were ready to leave.

"If I can I will try to send word," Kean told his parents "but please don't worry about us, we'll be safe with Tiggy and Og, I'm sure."

With tearful goodbyes, they set off through the morning mist down the hill in the direction of Dorcha Wood. The wind that buffeted Windy Hill Farm every night had stopped. Birds twittered in the hazel thicket as they followed Daione's Path into Dorcha Wood. They both wore rough spun grey breeches tucked into their boots and a knee length green

woollen tunic.

The sun's golden fingers reached across the pink sky and as they moved into the forest it darkened again, the air under the canopy of the ancient trees was warmer than that of the open fields.

"How is it father played in here as a child and yet at twenty this is the first time I have ventured this far?" Kean smiled.

"I guess father doesn't trust us like his father trusted him." A thought occurred to Allie. "Maybe after his encounter with the Faeries he thought it wouldn't be safe for his children to play in here."

"Hmm, you might have a point there." Kean checked around as though he expected angry Faeries to beset them. They couldn't help but jump at the sound of a creature scuttling away through the murky undergrowth.

****

Kean always wanted to be a warrior, to be the one who avenged the deaths of Allie's parents and his father's best friend. Kean had never forgotten the day Prince Alastor brought Allie to his family. He'd never forgotten the sadness as he watched the Leprechaun die in his father's arms. As a little boy, he hadn't understood the gravity of the Prince's wounds, nor the tragic events that had compelled him to seek out his childhood friend and beg his help to protect his daughter. Kean had grown restless on the farm and found it hard to take an interest when his father and Rían discussed crops and livestock. Rían seemed destined to marry a girl from the village and take over the farm. Plenty of girls in County Breaga would willingly marry Kean; he stood taller than average, broad shouldered and handsome. Most men his age were already married with children but Kean wanted adventure, he saw his destiny fighting for his homeland. Restoring Allie's people to Rois seemed a good place to start.

For thirty minutes, they followed the narrow, winding Daione's Path. Sometimes it turned back in the direction from which they had travelled; such was its rambling and convoluted course through the ancient woods. The trees grew thick and little light reached the forest floor. As they moved deeper into the woods, the undergrowth thinned until it disappeared and patches of ferns grew in its stead. Kean insisted he lead until they heard a familiar piercing scream followed by a sharp reprimand from a Leprechaun voice.

"Og!" Allie smiled.

"How did you know?"

Another ten paces they halted at a challenge.

"Put yer hands in the air and be showin' yerself!"

Kean glanced down at Allie and smiled. "It's us, Tiggy!"

"Your highness!" Tiggy trotted towards them, hatless and wearing a long woollen shirt; he hastened to pull on his boots. His red hair stood erect and gave the appearance of his head on fire. "I wasn't expecting yerself for hours yet, please accept my humble apologies for my state of unreadiness."

"Relax Tiggy." Allie smiled, "I'm in no hurry. Please—as you were."

An amused snort from Kean gained her attention and he raised an eyebrow. "Well commanded Your Royal Highness."

Kean winced as Allie kicked his ankle.

Another Leprechaun leaped onto the path, about to bow, he spotted Kean and straightened, his eyes wide.

"Ye didden mention we'd be travellin' wit' a giant!" He exclaimed staring at Kean. Of similar age to Tiggy, Willy had the same bright red hair and big blue eyes. Streaks of silver lined his red beard.

"Indeed I didn't!" said Tiggy. "Princess Alastríona, t'is is my manservant Ullian son of Ullian of Turloug. We call 'im Willy." Willy dressed quite differently to Tiggy. His raiment more the fashion of a high-ranking servant. The jewel encrusted Rose of Rois secured his double-breasted, green tunic at the shoulder. He wore dark brown leggings and black knee high boots with silver buckles. He had a black scarf around his neck and a green hat.

Willy removed his hat with a flourish and bowed to Allie.

"The giant's name is Kean O'Hara," Tiggy added.

Kean and Allie rested on a log at the edge of the Daione's Path while they waited for Tiggy and Willy. The forest lightened as the sun crept above the horizon.

"Manservant?" Willy's voice came from among the undergrowth. "If I'm to be ye manservant I'll be askin' fer wages."

Tiggy's inaudible reply came quickly and Willy snorted, his laughter tinkled through the ferns.

****

"Master Kean." Tiggy cleared his throat. Their quest now underway, once again they followed the narrow path. All carried packs except Og who trotted ahead and frequently rose high on his hind legs peering into the murky shadows of the ancient woods. "I didn't foresee yerself would be joinin' us on t'is journey. There will be places on our path where ye may be having difficulty wit' low hangin' branches." He coughed and muttered, "The Faeries may nary be likin' it t'either."

"Father told us about the Faeries." Allie turned to Tiggy. "Is there a way we can pass them without being seen?"

"Faeries are all seeing." Tiggy lowered his voice. "They're probably watchin' us now, there isn't a path through t'is end of Dorcha Wood they won't be havin' watched."

"Then surely, by the time we reach their village they will have had time to observe that I'm harmless," Kean declared.

Tiggy eyed the sharp iron axe secured to Kean's belt. "Faeries don't like iron. We'll 'ave to hide any iron we're carryin' inside our packs to keep it outta sight and well away from the Faeries. I'm nay sure they can't feel it, even from a distance."

Kean stopped, listened, and peered into the trees. "I can't shake the feeling we are being watched, perhaps you're right about the Faeries." He tossed a stick into the forest and they caught the sound of retreating feet scrambling away through the woods.

13

Glade Ceo

Late the following afternoon a heavy mist fell around them, it became difficult even to see Og leading them. Tiggy frowned and looked around as though he'd missed something. Og screamed and backed up, his mane standing on end.

Kean, Tiggy, and Willy formed a circle around Allie, their axes drawn and ready. Og hissed softly.

"Lower your weapons and we shall lower ours," came a voice out of the mist.

"Ye'll have t' be showin' yerself first!" called Tiggy.

"You're a long way from home for a Leprechaun, sir!" The voice now came from a point an arm's length away. "Why do three Leprechauns and a human trek through Faerie territory?"

"I weren't aware t'is end of the woods weren't open to all." Tiggy searched for where the voice came.

"You took great pains indeed to avoid the Faerie cities when you passed this way some days ago." The voice soft and wispy. "I'm wondering why you now find reason not to avoid us."

"We seek nothin' from ye', we are passin'." Tiggy pushed on, annoyed.

"The Fae have ever been friends to the Leprechauns, do you mean to say you've no wish to stop and honour that friendship?"

Tiggy drew a deep breath, his friendly face grew dark. "We…"

"Stand down, Aenghus!" Another voice came from the vanishing mist. A stern faced man—a Faerie, came striding towards them, frowning. Older than Kean, though not as old as Tiggy, he clapped his hands and a sullen Aenghus materialised. "I'll speak to you later about your rudeness, now go and see to it that my quarters are ready to house our guests." The last of the mist lifted to reveal a beautiful mound city. The Faerie bent and pressed his forehead to Og's, his hands resting on the sides of the grant's face, Og swished his tail.

"Good evening travellers, I am Maghnus. Welcome, Princess Alastríona, to Glade Ceo. Please accept my apologies for my guard's rudeness. Many of my people find it hard to relinquish the old ways."

The fog lifted on a cobblestoned square, a carved stone fountain splashed at the centre. Glade Ceo was a small but growing city. Newly laid stone paths wound their way between the mounds over which grew grass, ferns and bluebells. The doors and windows were made of wood surrounded by stone. Each mound had lush herbs growing outside the doors and windows.

Allie squeezed out between Kean and Tiggy, still in their defensive position. She addressed the Faerie.

"I'm pleased to meet you, Maghnus. These are my travelling companions, Tighearnan son of Tighearnan, Ullian son of Ullian and my adoptive brother, Kean O'Hara of County Breagha. I see you are already acquainted with Og."

Maghnus glanced at Kean and did a quick double take. He shook hands with the men then took Allie's hand and bowed. "Og the Defender of the Dorcha Grants," he smiled. "He has been a friend to the Fae for many long years."

"Og the Defender?" Tiggy cast a puzzled glance at Og.

"We bestowed that title upon him many years ago. Please, I'll have to ask you to put away your iron, I hope you won't mind—we Fae find it makes us weak. You'll have no need of it in Glade Ceo, for we would not harm you. In fact, we'd do anything to keep you from harm. We have watched you since you entered the forest, we cloaked our city until certain you weren't followed by anyone other than ourselves." He paused to study Allie a moment. "You are like your father Princess Alastríona. Prince Alastor was a good and brave Leprechaun."

"I hope I will learn to be as brave."

More Faeries emerged from the Mounds to stand behind Maghnus. The warriors, both male and female, wore a silvery-grey tunic overlayed by a long chain maille vest that shone silver, gold, and blue, with a jewelled bluebell in the centre of the breastplate. The Faeries were the same size as the Leprechauns with pointed ears, light brown skin and slanted eyes of green—some had eyes of brown or blue. Their spiky hair light brown and tipped with silver.

"We of Glade Ceo have monitored your childhood, Princess Alastríona, we have watched you grow. I helped Prince Alastor to take you to the O'Haras. You are more important to Dorcha Wood than you could imagine." Maghnus' eyes moved to Kean, "You are like your forefathers, Kean O'Hara, your family have for many generations been valuable allies to the folk of Dorcha Wood. Come, I will show you to my quarters, my kitchen is preparing a feast."

In the morning Allie awoke from a dream where Kean chased chattering and laughing Faeries around the Windy Hill Farmyard with an axe, he wore a silver maille tunic and a green hat. The smell of food brought her properly awake, her stomach rumbled. The chattering and laughing continued after she opened her eyes. She rose, dressed, and washed her face in the scented water provided. She found Kean, Tiggy, and Willy conversing with Maghnus in the dining room.

"Good morning your highness!" Maghnus bowed, "please allow my assistants to serve you."

In the centre of the room stood a table laden with pots and platters of food. A young Faerie girl curtsied and pulled out a chair for Allie to sit. Remembering Patrick's warning about thanking the Fae she said, "I appreciate your kindness."

Maghnus chuckled. "You have been warned of Fae customs I see. My efforts to convince the Fae to adopt a more sensible approach to other folk, was one reason among many for our exile from Glade Cloch. I believe there has been a softening of traditions there of late. So perhaps and I hope, you won't have too much difficulty."

He directed the Faerie girls to serve Allie breakfast. The girls wore dresses of shimmering fabric that gleamed all colours at once. They bustled around presenting bowls and platters. "The Fae have gained a bad reputation over the centuries," Maghnus continued, the vertical crease between his eyes gave him a stern appearance. "Our mysterious customs and rules of trade are too difficult for others to deal with. We found ourselves pushed to the edge of the forest community, the last to hear about issues of trade or diplomacy. These days, if you thank the exiled Faeries of Glade Ceo we will take it as gratitude, we won't think of it as intent to deceive. Old fashioned ideas must evolve if we are to move forward and have peace in Dorcha Wood."

Allie and her companions enjoyed breakfast served by the Faeries—sweet porridge, berries, fried eggs, and mushrooms served on fragrant yeast bread washed down with hot herbal tea.

When they finished breakfast, Maghnus brought out a maille cloak of the same material as his vest. "Wrap your iron in this and hide it in your pack." He presented the gift to Kean. "The Glade Cloch Fae won't feel its presence. Don't worry, it won't be heavy."

"Thanks! That's kind of you." Kean rose from the low seat.

They wrapped their iron weapons in the maille and to Kean's amazement his pack was no heavier than before.

"The Fae of Glade Ceo want very much for the Rois Leprechauns to return to their home city, for peace and the natural balance to return to Dorcha Wood." Maghnus stood with his hands on the back of his chair. "Ultan the Evil has declared himself Mayor of Rois, answering only to Idé Mae. They seek to gain control of the Leprechaun farmers along the River Síoga and the village of Turloug; luckily, not with any success, my spies tell me.

"I will do all I can to see my people restored to Rois, and I will try to do it as peacefully as I can," Allie hoped she didn't sound timid. "Ultan's services as Mayor will most certainly not be needed."

"That is music to my ears, Princess. My informants tell me a lot if not most of the Clurichauns in Rois have no desire to fight. Indeed it was only with the help of the Púcas that Ultan was able to take Rois and without them, I doubt he would hold it." Maghnus resumed his seat. "Don't believe all you hear about Clurichauns, they are barely different to Leprechauns, their one fault is they have no motivation to better themselves. They have a trusting nature. Mayor Ultan didn't earn the title of Ultan the Evil for no reason—I believe the Clurichaun's love of wine is how he has kept them loyal. He supplies them with an endless stream of alcohol which guarantees their fealty and keeps them under his power."

"Can you please tell us who the Púcas are?"

Tiggy spoke. "Púcas are Goblin-Faeries; they are shape-shiftin' creatures that live along the river from Kipper Hollow at a place called Púca Flats. They usually take the form of a goat like creature with a human body an' arms—an' the legs an' feet of a goat. They were harmless until Ultan the Evil promised them who-knows-what?"

"Ultan did not always live in Kipper Hollow?"

"No, I believe he arrived there from An Dara Choróin, a small village that we must pass on our journey to the Mountains of Fuar Lae. T'was the official city of the Clurichauns an age past, but there was a war an' most fled to Kipper Hollow. An Dara Choróin sits in the darkest part of Dorcha Woods."

"You would be wise to linger not in An Dara Choróin." Maghnus' green eyes fixed on Allie, "Goblins have taken control of the village and few Clurichauns remain. I believe there is a heavy infestation of Hobsnotters. We're not at war with them but in the past whenever Goblins have taken sides, it has been against the Leprechauns and the Fae. Goblins are vicious and stupid; in fact, the only thing they excel at is fighting and squabbling among themselves.

"You must be careful; Idé Mae will stop at nothing to keep the crown. She is responsible for the death of your parents and many others. You must remove her from Rois, the future of Dorcha Wood and beyond depends on it.

"You must protect Princess Alastríona with your lives." Maghnus looked from Kean to Tiggy. "We are all depending on her; there is no one else who can undertake this task."

Allie nodded, about to ask what Hobsnotters were when Tiggy spoke.

"Idé Mae will be given nary a chance to get at our Princess." Tiggy's blue eyes blazed, "The King entrusted myself wit' t'is mission and I mean to escort her to his side. An' I will do everyt'ing in my 'umble virtue to help her retake Rois."

"It is a great comfort to us that she has such stout and loyal company." Maghnus smiled at the Leprechaun's doughty face. "When you are ready to retake Rois the Fae will be there, to take your side. I will bring all the help I can muster. The Fae will watch over you until you leave Faerie country. My other spies will be watching too."

"We are grateful for your council and will accept any assistance offered to take back Rois." Kean touched his napkin to his lips. "It's good to know there'll be extra eyes watching for trouble." Kean got to his feet; his head brushed the ceiling.

"Now Allie, we must say good-bye to our friends and resume our journey."

The Glade Ceo Fae had replenished their packs with hard cheese, bread, and berry wine.

"Our spies will tell us when the time is right and we'll be there, the Fae will ever be the Leprechaun's closest allies." Maghnus told them as they waved good-bye, "Give my regards to Queen Madeléine."

There once was a radiant Faerie Queen,

sharp of wit and eyes of green·

Forced to the crown, ever shall she frown·

Alas! Would a seer have foreseen?

14

<u>Glade Cloch</u>

Once again, they trekked Daione's Path, Kean cursed softly each time he had to stoop under a low hanging branch; he muttered about having his axe stored away in his pack. The path wound off course to the north-west and back almost in the direction whence they'd travelled. On a bend they saw a tiny village, with shacks of stone and wood built among the trees. The smell of a pungent stew drifted in the air. A creature opened the door of a shack and stared for a few seconds then slammed it again.

"What was that?" Though Og hadn't screamed, Allie's skin prickled with fear.

"It's a Hobgoblin." Willy eyed the shack. "There's quite a few in these parts. They keep to themselves mostly."

"Are they the same as Goblins?" Kean was uneasy.

"Similar only in appearance, they smell a lot better too; they are friendly but often shy. They have powerful magic, said to be as powerful as dragons but they nary use it much at t'all."

Dorcha Wood grew darker as the path twisted and turned through the ancient trees. It wound its way around boulders—past rivulets and waterfalls, across stepping-stones in shallow streams and the occasional little bridge, sometimes wood, sometimes stone. Deer and rabbits grazed in glades of grass, brambleberries, and ferns. Insects hummed and fluttered in the last flowers searching for the sweet nectar within. On the edge of one of these glades they camped for the night, dining on rabbit roasted over the coals and Willy's fresh baked bread. Kean, Og, Tiggy and Willy shared the watch during the night, keeping the fire burning against the dark and cold. Allie wanted to share the watch but Tiggy scolded her and sent her to bed.

"I promised Patrick and the King I would be gettin' yerself to Fuar Lae safe an' well, so ye will be gettin' plenty of sleep an' nary any arguments!" Tiggy waggled a stern finger.

"Tiggy's right. Bed!" Kean pointed to her bedroll.

Allie wanted to protest but as soon as she lay down, weariness claimed her. Og curled up beside her and she pulled the blanket over both of them.

The next morning before sunrise, Og jarred them awake with a scream. Tiggy shouted his customary challenge and a small animal dashed away through the trees.

"A fox!" Tiggy sagged. He cast a reproachful glare in Og's direction and began preparations for the day ahead. Og bared his teeth in chagrin but his hackles stayed up for an hour.

As Allie tied her bedroll, she noticed a mouse-sized person watching her from where it sat astride a flower bud. Golden hair framed the tiny face and emerald green eyes. It wore blue overalls with a miniscule red hat. As she opened her mouth to say hello, it flew up into a tree, several others joined it, chattering and squeaking.

"Did you see that?" She looked around at the others.

"Yeah! What are they?" Kean rose and peered into the branches.

Tiggy laughed. "Ee-shees. Guardians of the woods, they protect the trees. The legends say they 'ave the most powerful magic of all—the gift of life. Unless you're a Faerie or a bird, ye should nary try flyin' in Dorcha Wood. They don't like it at t'all."

There were many questions Allie wanted to ask—about Goblins, Hobgoblins, Púcas, Hobsnotters, and now Ee-shees. Her mind raced, how many more creatures lived in the woods that she'd never heard of? How many might be potential enemies? She chastised herself for her paranoia and remembered her adoptive mother's wisdom, *'Hush, my darling, don't borrow silly worries from tomorrow.'*

In the dim morning light, they ate breakfast and set off along the path into the darkening forest. Clouds gathered overhead.

Mid-afternoon with a light rain falling they arrived at another Faerie city. Glade Cloch, like Glade Ceo, was a beautiful city made up of earth Mounds with stone frames around the doors and windows. There were mounds of different sizes, with wooden doors and glass windows in them, grass and ferns covered the roofs. Yellow daisies grew everywhere and birds sang in the trees; twisted branches arched overhead. The stone paths between the mounds looked ancient. Allie and her companions entered the Royal Court, which doubled as a town square.

"Kean! That statue looks like you." Allie pointed to the statue of a man standing poised for battle, his long sword ready for the attack. She read the words on the plinth, *'Máedóc Ó hEadhra'* and underneath *'Ego Resurget.'* Before they had time to wonder what this meant, a welcoming committee greeted them.

"Welcome to Glade Cloch Your Royal Highness, Princess Alastríona." They turned to face an imperious Faerie woman. "Indeed, we have been expecting you for some time. I am Madeléine, Queen of Glade Cloch." Her abrupt manner made the travellers feel tardy at arriving so late. "I see you have brought with you that nefarious scoundrel O'Hara, the one who most ungraciously refused to hand you over to our care. I

sincerely hope his lack of manners has not rubbed off on you."
She eyed Allie with distaste, assuming his lack of manners
would of course rub off on her. Kean opened his mouth to
protest his innocence but Allie spoke up before he could
further incur her wrath.

"I am pleased to meet you, Your Majesty." She stepped forward. "This is my adoptive brother Kean O'Hara, son of Patrick of County Breagha, and these are Tighearnan son of Tighearnan of Turloug and Ullian son of Ullian of Turloug and Og the Defender."

"The son of O'Hara, I see." She squinted at Kean for a moment and continued, "You take after your father," she accused and turned her eyes back to Allie. "Three of your companion's passed by Glade Cloch under the cover of darkness last week" Madeléine surveyed Tiggy, Willy, and Og down the length of her nose, "We suspected they were on their way either to you or to those self-proclaimed rebels of Glade Ceo." Her mouth pinched at this statement as though to prevent more words of these fell deeds to escape.

"Please be accepting our 'umblest apologies for our turrible lack of courtesy," Tiggy's voice trembled, "The king gave us orders to move swiftly to bring the Princess to his side."

"The King!" Madeléine hissed and looked Tiggy over in a hope to find a fault in his appearance. "Surely he is not still claiming to be king? That creature, Idé Mae is in possession of his crown and his palace."

"She won't for too much longer." Allie's voice held a strength she didn't feel in her heart. The haughty Faerie queen posed a frightening figure and with what she knew of the Glade Cloch Faeries, might be easily offended. Allie held her head high and met the queen's eyes. "Well, it has been a pleasure to meet you, Queen Madeléine, but we must keep moving. We have many miles to cover."

"You will stay." Madeléine snapped her fingers and a group of subordinates appeared. "Make our guests welcome! They shall be staying with us this night. Instruct the kitchens to prepare a feast and see it is of the highest standard! Anrie! Show the Princess and her aids to the guest quarters. And make sure the Grant is well cared for." She waved a hand in Og's direction, turned and with nose aloft, disappeared through the door of the Royal Mound followed by a her maidservant.

"We could run," suggested Kean.

"We can't afford to offend her."

"She's already offended and I think she's enjoying it."

The guest quarters were comfortable, Kean had to bend to go through the doors but once inside could stand straight.

They freshened up and the butler showed them to the Queens dining room and made a fuss of Kean.

"I hope you will be most comfortable there, sir." Anrie straightened the cutlery. "We've not had a visit from one of the big folk for many a long year."

"I'm perfectly comfortable, thank you." Kean sat on a low, cushioned stool.

As the Queen had commanded, the feast was delicious. The Faeries waited on the travellers with a diligence born of abject terror of their Queen. Her sharp tongue recommenced the verbal lashing once dinner had ended. She demanded Allie's non-existent battle plan and slated her lack of preparedness.

"My cousin was negligent indeed to allow such a motley band of miscreants to seize his kingdom," Madeléine declared. "It wouldn't have happened if he hadn't rejected my father's offer to supply an army of well-trained Fae to guard the city of

Rois, but no—" She took another dainty sip of her berry wine. "He was poorly advised by his Viceroy. My King father had the same dilemma with his own Viceroy at the time. Men do not make good kings, this you'd do well to remember."

This last piece of advice puzzled Allie. *Would they be better as queens?* Then she realised what the Queen had said.

"Your cousin?" She frowned.

Madeléine snorted, "You've been poorly schooled in your family's royal history I see. I might have known." She cast a malevolent glance at Kean. "Yes, the king's mother was my grandfather's sister. When your great great-grandfather seized the throne from his brother—my great-grandfather the King of Glade Cloch insisted that in order for continuing co-operation from the Fae, the King of Rois should marry his son Cillian to my dear, great aunt Isabelle."

Allie glanced at Tiggy who shrugged. "I guess that would explain ye Faerie like magical ability—and yer unusual hair. I was nary aware of a connection but—well, I'm just an 'umble man-at-arms."

Madeléine's dainty sips became less so until they were more the fashion of gulping and slurping. She harangued and lectured on everything from the disorganisation of the Leprechauns of Rois to the lack of courtesy and decorum of Maghnus. "He cast aside his royal obligations! And don't get me schtarted!" She took another gulp of wine—her eyes searched around the table and fixed Allie with a myopic stare. "Schtarted!" she hiccoughed. "On the badgers! I'll not schtand for their rudeness! Allied themselves with Maghnus, theyohme! Oh yesh! *hic* They owe me immesshurably." She finished with a delicate burp.

Allie realised she stared in astonishment and averted her eyes; they fell upon the young Faerie who sat across the table from her and Allie blushed. She had the feeling he had been watching her. He grinned and winked, a wicked twinkle lit his eyes.

"Now she's got that off her chest she'll be off to her bed any minute," he whispered.

"I heard your rude remark young Nyvián," piped the Queen, "your impertinence is only exsheeded by you superior jousting *hic* ability! Which is just ash well or I'd dishinherit you." She held out an unsteady hand to the maidservant who watched attentively. "Take me to my bedchamber, Moyna darling, there's a goog-url."

They watched her leave, helped by her devoted servant. An embarrassed silence prevailed for a few moments.

"So!" Nyvián grinned and clapped his hands. "Now Aunt Maddy has left perhaps we can discuss your strategy for retaking Rois from the Toad Queen."

He had the most captivating green eyes Allie had ever seen, she blushed whenever he smiled. He wore a tunic of the same silvery fabric Maghnus had worn, along with the maille vest that shone silver, gold and blue. A yellow-jewelled daisy shone on his breastplate. Allie saw Kean smirk at her out of character shyness.

"Any help or advice ye can be givin' us will be most appreciated," Tiggy raised his cup to his lips. "Getting into Rois an' ousting Idé Mae and 'er minions will be hard enough; the city is guarded like a prison. But we must be getting to Fuar Lae first and I'm worried at what might be waitin' fer us, 'specially since the only road I know to Fuar Lae is Caonach Road which runs right past Rois. I know nothing of the Troll Road that leads up Tarragon Mountain and even if we went that way I don't know if there is a road from there to Fuar Lae." Tiggy sighed; he took a drink from his cup and set it back on the table.

"Og the Defender is a good guide," Nyvián's eyes moved from Allie to Tiggy. "If you decide to take a different route I'm sure he would guide you well. I'm no expert on the subject but I know there is folk living on Tarragon Mountain and I believe it is where Orla resides these days as well."

"Who is Orla?" Allie once again felt her ears turning as red as her hair when Nyvián looked at her and smiled.

What's wrong with me?

"Orla is a golden dragon who was once allied with Rois but when old King Angus the Erratic was tyrannizing the folk along the River Síoga, Orla flew away to the mountain in disgust and took with him his magic. He cursed himself never to return until the hand of peace once again ruled in the Four Kingdoms."

"He cursed himself?" Allie frowned, "Why would he curse himself?"

"To prevent himself intervening in the affairs of Dorcha Wood—or so I'm told. Orla won't stand for the inhabitants of Dorcha Wood fighting amongst themselves and more's the pity, he won't allow the dragons to become involved in any of our wars. I don't know if there were efforts to bring him back when Treasach deposed Angus, it happened well before my time. I fear a lot of knowledge is lost to my generation after the invasion of Rois. My elders tell me there is a vast library in the Palace, I hope it has survived Idé Mae's regime.

"Dorcha Wood was a peaceful community until Idé Mae came along. It was called Quattuor Regna Vidisset Unitum— or Four Kingdoms United."

"Four kingdoms?"

"Leprechauns, Clurichauns, Faeries, and Elves. I'm not sure where the Elves come in to it, I've read they were allied to the Leprechauns but can't find any other useful information. The inhabitants of Dorcha Wood have withdrawn from each other since the invasion of Rois."

For hours they discussed their options until Tiggy saw Allie suppress a yawn and demanded she retire for the night. "We've a long way to be goin' tomorrow."

"You're going tomorrow?" Nyvián's eyes found Allie's, "I mean, surely you could stay one more day and rest."

Kean grinned. "I'm sure you will get to see my sister again before too long."

Nyvián blushed this time. Allie, a brand new shade of bright red, brought a yelp from Kean as she kicked his foot.

"And my aunty—um the Queen I'm sure would love to have you stay a while longer." Nyvián tried to cover his embarrassment.

As Nyvián accompanied them to their quarters, Kean asked if Queen Madeléine had a husband.

"No, she never married. There's a rumour she almost did but her intended stood her up at the altar and ran off with a Hobsnotter princess, but it's just a rumour."

Allie wanted to ask about Hobsnotters, but his smile rendered her speechless.

Allie found herself unable to fall asleep for the first time in her life, she kept seeing Nyvián's green eyes and dazzling smile, each time she felt a swirly swooping sensation in her stomach as though she'd missed a step.

In a place of beauty and bloom,

in the air floats sweet perfume·

Together they lie, their one child to cry,

for lives ended in days of doom·

15

<u>The Tombs of Glade Cloch</u>

Allie and her companions woke at first light. The Queen's butler, Anrie, accompanied them to the great hall for breakfast. As they took their seats, Kean looked past Allie and grinned. Allie turned to see what amused her brother and saw Nyvián standing in the door, searching the room for—

"Ah!" he smiled, "Allie! There you are." He sat beside her.

She blushed and the butterflies in her stomach destroyed her appetite.

"I hope you don't mind me calling you Allie?"

Kean smirked, pretending to focus on the plate before him.

103

"No." Allie's voice almost failed her. "Not at all, in fact I rather prefer it." Nobody before had made her this nervous.

Nyvián grinned. "Breakfast!" he declared as a troop of servants arrived bearing platters of food and lay them on the table.

"The Queen is not breakfasting with us?" Allie had dreaded facing the Queen again.

"It's a bit early for my aunt, but I daresay she'll be up in time to see you off with loads more advice." He reached for a bowl of fruit and offered it to her. Allie took a peach and put it on her plate. She attempted to eat it but gave up and put it aside.

"Nyvián, I would like to visit the tomb of my parents which I believe is here at Glade Cloch. Would you show me where they are?"

"Yes, we can go now if you finished your breakfast?" He looked at the peach which had a few nibbles taken from it and raised an eyebrow. "You're welcome to accompany us." Nyvián turned to Kean. "Your father was a good friend of

Prince Alastor's I believe, so I'm sure he'll be pleased to know you'd paid your respects."

The Mounds that housed the tombs bore little difference on the outside to the others of Glade Cloch but inside they were majestic. The huge marble columns rose to a high ceiling centred by an ornate dome with stained glass windows to allow light from outside. Golden daisies decorated the polished white floors.

"They're here." Nyvián led Allie and Kean to a white stone tomb with the pink rose of Rois on the door. An inscription written in gold letters read:

'*Whither Goest Thou Beidh Mé a Leanúint.*'

"It means, 'Where you go, I will follow'."

Allie couldn't speak. Kean sank to a nearby plinth and took her hand in his. She wept for the parents of whom she had no memory, their young lives taken by villainy and greed. They sacrificed all for her. Nyvián comforted her with an arm around her shoulders. Since the previous night, Nyvián had joined Kean as one of the two most important people in her life. She gave in to the strain of the past week—fear of what lay ahead, this journey was not a jaunt and life had taken a turn over which she had no control. As her sobs subsided, Allie became aware of Nyvián's arms around her, her face rested against his chest. Kean had wandered across the wide hall pretending to read the inscription on another tomb.

"They had their whole lives ahead of them," Allie whispered. "It's so unfair. If I could speak to them for a few moments, perhaps I'd learn what to do. I'm just one girl and I've never done anything courageous. I don't know if I can do this, I know nothing of fighting wars. I have no army—how do I build such an army? I know so little of Dorcha Wood and its inhabitants."

"You're not alone you know," Nyvián whispered. "Glade Cloch will send assistance when you're ready to make a move on Idé Mae. I will have my people watching."

"Maghnus of Glade Ceo has also offered to send help." Allie worried this would change his mind, given the animosity between the two Faerie communities.

"I'm aware of my father's offer; I'll have to do my best to provide you with a bigger and better army than his." The cheeky smile had returned.

"Your father?"

"Yes, Maghnus is my father. He left Glade Cloch when I was a small child but my mother and I stayed. My mother was not strong. She died when I was three, so Aunt Madeléine watched over me with the help of her companion, Moyna." His arms held her close; his breath tickled her ear. "I've never spent more than a few days with my father. He's the rightful heir to the crown of Glade Cloch."

This insight into Nyvián's childhood made Allie forget her woes. "Now I know that, I can see you are like Maghnus, though he's more serious than you are."

"Being raised by my aunt has taught me not to take life too seriously. If I suffered she and my father's constant squabbling without seeing the humour in it I'd have gone mad years ago." He stood back frowning, his hands on Allie's shoulders studying her tearful face. "After seeing such tragedy as I know the both of them have, you would think as brother and sister they would value one another more."

The travellers set off mid-morning along Daione's Path, back into the depths of Dorcha Wood. Allie knew she didn't fool Kean as she walked head down in front her companions, tailing Og. She hid the tears and cherished a secret wish she and Nyvián would be together again in less troubled times. The good-byes had taken longer than expected as Madeléine weighed them down with gifts and stern council, though the nature of the gifts given left them awe-struck. She had presented Tiggy and Willy each a silver dagger in a sheath of leather. She gave Allie a silver sword, the hilt inlaid with the pink jewelled Rose of Rois.

"Kean O'Hara, I give to you *Argent Storm—Defender of the Dorcha Realm.* It is an ancient sword of the big people, entrusted to the Fae long ago. Your adopted sister will need support in her quest to restore peace to Dorcha Wood." She'd raised an imperious eyebrow at Allie. "Use it wisely, Kean O'Hara."

Allie had thought, judging by the pinched mouth, Madeléine doubted he would. The Fae fitted them with Faerie maille vests of the same material as the cloak Kean had kept hidden in his pack with their iron inside. Nyvián had taken

Allie to one side, drew a long silver chain from his pocket and slipped it over her head. "I can't promise this has any magical qualities or anything, but I hope when you wear it you'll think of me sometimes."

The chain had a small pendant of yellow jewels set in the shape of a daisy. Allie wanted to cry, she had never wanted to leave that beautiful place.

"Of course I'll think of you and I'll wear it all the time."

Her thoughts clung to Nyvián as she trekked Daione's Path, all the while she moved further from him. He'd kissed her but once and Allie knew that moment would stay with her forever.

****

Watching from the cover of the forest a hooded figure seethed with anger. Its hand grasped the wooden staff in murderous rage.

In Dorcha Wood, a slipshod town

that never sought to wear the crown·

Their lives were shady, then came a lady,

with vice and malice a King brought down·

16

The Cursed Faerie

As they moved into Clurichaun territory, the path became unkempt; the bridges derelict and falling down. Large tree roots grew across the path and created obstacles. They passed by abandoned farmhouses, barns, and moss covered stone walls. Fields of berries where the vines grew wild, had been unattended for many years—the forest had almost reclaimed fields once used for cropping.

They sheltered for the night under the dense forest canopy out of sight of the path. Now out of Faerie Country they took heed and lit no fire.

"We'll be passin' through An Dara Choróin tomorrow." Tiggy waved his hand at a raven that cawed in the tree above them. Kean threw a stick at it and it flew off, quorking angrily. "We must nary linger there an' Allie we must be disguisin' yerself." Tiggy glanced at Og and shook his head. "Grants are only ever seen with nobility."

"What's the point of disguising Allie," Kean grinned, "when you have me stalking along with a big sword and standing out like a sore thumb?"

"Good point." Allie eyed Kean's sword. "Perhaps we can put a rope around your neck and pretend we've captured you."

Kean raised a thoughtful eyebrow.

Cold rain fell as they passed through the bleak and grimy village of An Dara Choróin. They wore their hoods pulled tight over their head to cover their red Leprechaun hair. An ancient stone castle stood abandoned, trees and vines grew among the broken masonry. Only the legs remained of a statue that once stood on the moss-cover plinth in the town square. Shadowy figures with shrouded eyes watched from out of doors and dark alleys between the buildings that crowded close together as if to hold one another upright. Kean limped barefooted through the muddy main street, bent over under the weight of his pack, a convincing performance. He carried Willy's cooking utensils and as much other stuff they could squeeze in—they gave Kean the extra burden of firewood with his sword secreted inside. He wore a torn shirt with dirt rubbed in to give the appearance of a desperate captive. They used a piece of charcoal to give him a black eye and facial bruising. Tiggy, his face and cloak coated in muck, held the rope tied around Kean's neck. He shook a stick as he growled insults and empty threats. Og pretended to be a wild Grant captured by Willy and dragged against his will with a rope on his halter. Og liked this game and made Willy's job hard work, he leaned back and dug in his heels, his tail swished from side to side. Willy sweated and cursed as he hauled on the rope. Allie remembered the Faerie part of her ancestry, faded into the background and passed unseen. Her heart thudded as inhospitable eyes watched them pass. Her life had never before depended on her ability to turn invisible; in fact, she had doubted she could manage it in the presence of danger.

They congratulated themselves once past the town and washed the dirt off themselves, Kean put his boots and cloak back on. They redistributed the load from Kean's pack and removed the rope from Og's halter. As they did the night before, they camped well away from Daione's Path and lit no fires—which was a pity, Kean pointed out, given he'd carried a load of firewood for half a day.

****

In the pitch of midnight, Kean sat first watch. He heard rustling a short distance south of their camp, the sound of feet shuffling through the leaf litter on the forest floor. Kean groped around and shook Tiggy and Willy awake.

"There are things moving around out there," he whispered. He felt Og brush past him. "I'm going to have to light a firebrand. Phew! What's that smell?"

The combined smell of unwashed feet, sweat and an old latrine drifted in from the direction of the sounds.

"Goblins! I smell Goblins!" Tiggy's voice shook in the dark.

114

As the firebrand flickered to life, Og rushed back past Kean and screamed. Kean turned to see what had alerted the Grant and at first he saw nothing. Then his stomach lurched.

"No!" His panicked cry seemed to come from someone else. "Allie!"

Allie had disappeared from her bed. He ran in circles searching for her, bile rose in his throat. During the distraction, someone had taken her. Distraught, Kean, Tiggy, Willy and Og searched the woods for hours but found no sign of her. White faced and inconsolable—the pain in Kean's chest restricted his breathing. Using the wood he'd carried that day, he lit a blazing fire and began searching for tracks. He found large footprints in the area from where the scuffling sounds came and used the firebrands to follow. They made slow progress trailing the tracks over leaf litter and logs through the woods at night but they pressed on, Kean followed the lingering stench as much as the footprints.

****

Allie awoke from a deep sleep, cold air and the leaves of trees brushed her face, someone carried her, someone who flew fast. She couldn't see who carried her but knew she'd never met him before. She struggled and kicked.

"Put me down!" She squealed and punched at her captor. "Where are you taking me?"

She knew a male carried her, a strong male Faerie. He didn't speak as he continued flying high over the forest and descended into the tree tops, Allie squealed again as they plunged toward the ground. He set her down and tied her hands and feet. Allie scanned the area, a fire burned in a circle of stones. A large cooking pot lay on its side on the ground of the rough camp; the tracks of big feet cockled the soiled around the flickering fire. Her captor was indeed a Faerie of about Maghnus' age, although his shabby clothing and unkempt appearance was not a look of either of the Faerie cities. He had a tooth missing to one side of his mouth and a chip from another. A long scar furrowed one side of his face, running from cheekbone to chin, and his nose had a broken heal to it. He had a sparse head of silver dishevelled hair on his head. The top of his left ear was missing and gave his head a lopsided appearance. He dropped Allie's satchel on the ground beside her, sat on a nearby rock and waited.

"Who are you? Why have you kidnapped me?"

He didn't answer but studied her, his battered face troubled. He checked around, tilted his head and listened. Allie's heart pounded, she trembled and shivered in the cold damp air. Never before had she been anywhere without a member of her family somewhere close by.

The shabby Faerie jumped to his feet; somebody approached. He glanced at Allie, held a forefinger to his lips and shook his head. A group of creature came out of the trees, Allie counted twelve—bigger than Leprechauns and Faeries but not as tall as humans, they had large heads and big pointed ears. They had slanted black eyes and high cheek bones. Their feet and hands were twice as long as those of a human and on the tips of their long fingers and toes they had black claw-like nails. They wore a toga made from animal skins; each carried a spear and a heavy wooden club. These creatures had to be Goblins—Goblins topped her list of feared creatures.

The biggest of them slouched over to Allie, he spoke in a gruff guttural tongue and the Faerie replied in the same language pointing at the ropes holding Allie's wrists and ankles. The Goblin crouched in front of Allie and stared. He sniffed her and reached out with a long, calloused hand.

"Pruddy!" He bared his fearsome teeth in a travesty of a smile; his heavy hand patted her head and moved down to her shoulder. "Verr pruddy!"

Allie's eyes watered from the smell of his unwashed body and she recoiled, terror coursed through her veins. She used her elbow to shove his hand away and hoped Kean would find her soon, for she was sure he searched. She recoiled at a squeaking and chattering close to her ear, it was an Ee-shee, another and another landed on her shoulders squeaking and shaking tiny fists at the Goblin. Two of the little creatures flew at him screeching fiercely, shooting sparks at his eyes and stinging his face. He reeled back as one would from a venomous spider. To Allie's relief he lost interest and hobbled, bow-legged back to the fire where his kinfolk gathered. They threw wood on the fire until it burned high, curled up beside it like dogs, and fell asleep.

"Thank you." Allie whispered to the Ee-shees. She didn't know if they understood but silently thanked them for their intervention. They flew into the branches of a nearby tree.

The Faerie made a grunting noise and Allie studied him. His eyes shut tight and his hands clenched in front of him, his wrist pressed together. He tried to speak but couldn't form the words.

Allie was about to speak when he spluttered, "P – Prin – cess— uh—I—s—soh—ree."

Allie stared; those few words had exhausted him.

"Uh—I—cursed. C—cannot s—peak."

"You're cursed?" Allie whispered. He nodded.

"T—two—d—days ago—I—speak—first—time—man—y—years." He puffed with exertion. "Ch—chains—o—on—me."

"Where are you from?" Allie glanced at the Goblins.

"G–Gla..."

"You're from Glade Cloch?"

Again, he nodded.

"But you spoke to the Goblin." She watched as he nodded again. "You said two days ago you began to speak again—in your own language?"

He looked into her eyes and nodded.

Allie checked the sleeping Goblins. "Do you think the spell is lifting?"

Again he nodded.

"And they had you chained?"

This time he shook his head. "M—Mag—ic ch—chains."

Allie glanced at his hands and feet, he did have a curious habit of holding them as though bound by a short chain and when he walked, he shuffled.

"O—oh—only Roy – al Fae can—b—break. I—slave."

"Who are you a slave to? The Goblins?" Allie didn't think Goblins had such powerful magic that they could chain someone with a spell. The Faerie confirmed her notion as he once again shook his head.

"C—can't s—say n—name.

"So Queen Madeléine could break the chains?" Talking to him had calmed Allie a little; she didn't shake as much. She cast a glance at the Goblins.

"O—or—Magh—nus, any with r—roy—al Fae blood."

"Oh"

Is this a trick? Does he know I have royal Faerie blood?

"What is your name?"

"F—Fer—ghus."

"Ferghus?"

"Y—y—" he nodded.

Allie jumped with fright as the Goblins sprang to their feet jabbering and sniffing the air. She could hear the sound of more feet drawing near. A small group of Goblins joined the rest at the fire, chattering and babbling. The one who had worried her earlier approached Allie again. She shrunk back as he leaned down, but instead of touching her, he grabbed her satchel. He opened it and pulled out the box. It tinkled as he held it close to his face, examining it, turning it over and sniffing. When it wouldn't open, he dropped it on the ground; his long, grubby fingers reached back inside the bag and pulled out the cittern. He raised it to his face and sniffed it.

Givvus zat!" Another Goblin saw the shining instrument and slouched over. The first turned away, ducking his head and lifting one grubby shoulder to shield his prize. He cradled the cittern and hunched his back, trotted on tiptoes to a log and sat, grinning in anticipation. He plucked the strings and it rewarded him with a dull discordant humming sound. The Goblins around the fire laughed raucously at his dismal failure.

His adversary charged, "Givvus zat! Giv—"

The would-be musician swung the Cittern and smacked him across the forehead. Allie cringed but her precious instrument remained unscathed. The two rivals took to fighting; they tossed the cittern aside in favour of a more familiar pursuit. They punched and kicked, climbed onto the log and dived on one another with savage body-slams. The rest of the Goblins gathered around, they laughed and growled, occasionally they scattered as the combatants rolled too close.

"Urgh oough!" They chanted and beat their chests and stamped their feet.

A smaller Goblin picked up the cittern, sniffed it and approached Allie with a wide, snaggle-toothed grin.

"Pruddy murk?" He passed her the instrument. "Vupper grudder, murk! Pruddy murk!" When he saw Allie's tied hands he waffled a few words at Ferghus who shuffled over and untied them.

"He wants me to play it?" Allie asked the Faerie. Ferghus nodded.

With shaking hands, Allie began to play. As she played, she hoped the cittern would have the same effect on the Goblins as it did on the farmyard animals at home. The Goblins lost interest in the brawl and listened, even the brawlers stopped and sat on the log, gazing into the fire, their arms around one another's shoulders. On and on Allie played, she was about to give up when she noticed a few large heads beginning to nod, one by one they curled up on the ground and went to sleep. As she played, she spoke to Ferghus.

"If you want your freedom, untie me. I would be most grateful if you would help me find my companions."

"B—But h—ow—?" Ferghus looked puzzled.

"You'll have to swear fealty to me, the Leprechauns and the Fae." She continued playing random chords on the cittern.

Ferghus nodded. He fell to his knees in front of her and gazed into her eyes. "I—swear—a—all—ways. I—I am F—Fae b—born."

Playing open strings one handed, she lay her free hand on his head and hoping it would work, she intoned, "I free you from the spell."

Ferghus fell face down into the leaf litter; Allie feared he might be unconscious. She resumed playing the cittern and worried her attempt at magic had failed. She prodded the Faerie with her bound feet. He moved and awoke to his surroundings. He got to his knees and held his hands in front of his face. He stretched his arms wide, laughed and jumped to his feet, kicking his legs out one at a time.

"Thank you! Your Royal Highness, thank you! But how? You're not a Faerie."

"You'd be surprised, now can you untie my feet, please?"

"Certainly!" Ferghus touched the rope and it fell away from her ankles. "It was just a Faerie knot."

"I wish I'd known that a few hours ago. Now do me a favour and pick up that box and put it in the satchel? We're going to have to move quickly, once the Goblins can no longer hear music they will most likely wake up."

"You're forgetting we Faeries are powerful flyers. If you will allow me, climb on my back and we'll be on our way."

Allie put the cittern back into her satchel and climbed on to his back. The Goblins stirred, a few jumped to their feet. As

Ferghus lifted into the air, he grunted in pain and dipped back toward the ground.

"I've been hit!" A Goblin spear had pierced the Faeries ribs. Another hissed past them so close Allie felt the air move on her face. The Ee-shee crowded around, their voices shrilled encouragingly. In her terror, she willed Ferghus to fly away and felt him gain altitude again, they lifted high over the trees and away from the Goblin camp, the harsh cries fading in the dark. Allie felt Ferghus slipping and discovered it was she who kept them airborne. She renewed her grip on the Faerie and focused, she flew effortlessly, yet even in her frantic state of mind, she marvelled at her new found ability to fly. The Guardians of the Wood swarmed, their tiny lanterns guided her through the dark.

In the dim early morning, shivering with cold, Allie spotted a fire in the trees far below. She wove her way down through the forest canopy following the Ee-shees, landed beside a large tree and set Ferghus on the damp ground. The Ee-shees crowded around him squeaking to one another in urgent tones. She crept over and peered around the trees.

Tiggy and Willy sat on a log. She couldn't see anyone else and was about to call out when a familiar high pitched scream startled her so, she almost fell to her knees. The Eeshees squeaked and scattered in alarm.

"Og!" She'd failed to see the Grant standing in the shadows a few steps away.

"Allie!" Kean ran from the trees behind Tiggy and Willy, "Allie!" Kean scooped his sister into a tight hug. "Where have you been? We thought the Goblins had taken you, we followed their tracks but we lost them here."

While Willy attended the wound in Ferghus' ribs, Allie told them, punctuated by outraged curses from Kean, what had happened.

"So we need to get moving quickly." Allie glanced nervously into the darkened woods. "They could find us at any moment."

"T'is man can nary be moved," said Willy, "I've removed the spear but he's gravely wounded." He waved at the Ee-shees as they swarmed around the wounded and bleeding Ferghus.

"No!" Allie raised a hand. "Leave them, I think they want to help."

She watched the Ee-shees as they formed a circle around the wound. They held their hands in the air over the hole in the Faerie's side and their tiny voices began a chant, the sing-song crooning grew louder. Ferghus glowed as a shimmering silver mist formed over the wound, it swirled—slowly at first then faster and faster, down in a vortex and vanished into his body. As they watched, the glow faded until it extinguished over the wound; the firebrand in Kean's hand the only light. The Guardians of the Woods fell exhausted to the ground. Ferghus sat up and looked around.

"Ee-shee magic!" Tiggy's beard twitched with excitement. "I've heard stories but never been seeing it fer m'self."

One by one, the Ee-shees recovered and flew away into the morning sky, their voices faded.

"Thank you!" Allie called.

Og led them back to where they'd camped the night before and they prepared to say good-bye to Ferghus.

"Fifteen years ago, I left Glade Cloch to move to Glade Ceo to join my family when I was captured by the Goblins and cursed b—b," he sighed. He still could not name the one who had cursed him. "This time I hope I can make it safely. My family thinks I'm dead. I am forever in your debt Princess, you freed me from a living hell. One last thing," he added glancing from Kean to Allie, "Beware the r—red f—fox. I can't tell you anymore but t—things are n—not always w—what they seem." He held out his hand for Kean to shake.

"The red fox. Thanks for the warning," Kean shook his hand.

Beware the red fox? His words mystified Allie.

"Give our regards to Maghnus." Allie, Tiggy and Willy shook hands with the shabby Faerie.

"Poor old Ferghus." Kean gazed after the Faerie. "He's had a hard time of it. Can you imagine putting up with Goblin stink for fifteen years?"

****

129

Upon hearing of the shabby Faerie's arrival in Glade Ceo, Maghnus asked to speak with him and listened in stunned silence as Ferghus told his story. Weeks after Madeléine had assumed the throne of Glade Cloch she granted an appeal to the servant convicted of Chamberlain Martok's murder.

"They overturned my sentence and set me free." He told Maghnus of the Goblins, the evil curse that robbed him of his native tongue and bound him with invisible chains.

"Who was it that cursed you?" Maghnus asked.

Ferghus could still not utter the name.

"A witch? Is the witch still a threat?" Maghnus pressed on.

The tired but determined Ferghus nodded.

"The Goblins are under h—h—they are controlled. We must help the Princess to take back the Leprechaun Kingdom. We must bring back the peace to the folk of Dorcha Wood."

His youth was stolen and his honour taken,

an unjust verdict saw freedom forsaken·

But hope comes forward with a fabled sword,

Chains break, the curst voice reawakens·

17

Og's Detour

As Allie's party entered a ferny grove, Og screamed, before Tiggy could shout a challenge the ferns around Og erupted, dozens of rat sized creatures poured from the greenery and attacked him. Their strident voices set up a cacophony as Og kicked and bit at them. His companions charged into the fray, kicking and swinging axe and hammer. Allie saw one of the creatures up close as it charged, teeth and claws bared, a dirty green-skinned individual—human in shape but with coarse, bristly hair that stood erect. His long pointed nose bowed over his mouth; his forehead broad and wrinkled, the expression lines followed the curve of his eyebrows; his eyes muddy brown and bloodshot. Allie smacked him on his shoulder with her hammer, he shrieked and tried to attack again, but Kean's boot sent him flying into the ferns. Abruptly as they had begun, they abandoned the attack and ran screeching and whooping into the woods.

As Allie checked her companions, her eyes fell upon a badger standing head to head with Og—they pressed their foreheads together for a few moments before the badger loped off down the path from where they'd trekked. As Allie sat on a log to repack her satchel, she caught a glimpse of a dark creature scampering out of the badger's path and into the forest.

Og trotted to Allie, his large brown eyes on hers. Closer he came and pressed his forehead against Allie's—the forest around her fell silent.

A voice echoed in her head:

'Please Princess, we must not continue on this path. The Fae spies of Glade Ceo sent the badger, Ted the Heroic. He has warned me another bigger ambush awaits us if we do.'

But where shall we go? I cannot turn back.

'Do you trust me?'

Yes, I trust you with our lives.

'You must follow me, no matter where I lead you.'

Allie inhaled.

Yes, lead us dear Og. We will follow. Wherever you lead.

Og trotted off Daione's Path and led them south into the forest. Allie followed, weaving her way through the ferns and into the trees.

"Come quickly!" she called to the others as they scrambled to pick up their dropped packs.

"Allie! Where are we going? What was that about?" Kean fired questions as he and the others ran to catch up. "Did Og talk to you?"

"Yes, we must follow him."

"I hope he knows where he's going," Kean picked his way through the ferns and tree roots and ducked the low hanging branches.

"Og's kind has been trackers of the forest folk for t'ousands of years," Tiggy panted following close behind Kean, "they 'ave wandered Dorcha Wood from end to end since time began. He gets a wee over excited wit' bein' our look-out but you can be sure he knows where he's goin'."

Their trail darkened as they ran further into the forest. For hours, they forced their way through trees and rocks and finally spilled out onto a narrow rocky path that took them into higher and rougher terrain.

Og halted and hissed, his hackles erect. Kean stepped in front of Allie and he slid his sword from its scabbard. Tiggy raised his axe. Ahead, a Goblin perched on a rock beside the path.

"Ugh! Yuck!" Kean drew back. The smell of the Goblin greased it way to their nostrils, but worse than the smell—the Goblin had his finger deep in his nose, mining for boogers. Up to the second knuckle of his long index finger, he twisted and delved—his pinkie finger extended in the manner of a lady sipping tea from a fine china cup. He withdrew his finger, sniffed it and held his find inches from his eyes, they crossed as he focussed on the nose crumb—satisfied he stored it in a little leather bag that hung around his neck on a string.

Allie slipped the cittern from her satchel and began to play, gradually increasing the volume.

"What are you doing?" Kean whispered.

Allie's heart quickened as the Goblin's head turned and he sniffed the air searching for the source of the music. The travellers didn't move a muscle; Allie kept behind Kean. Soon the Goblin relaxed, curled up on the rock, inserted his finger into his nostril and fell asleep. A problem arose that Allie hadn't foreseen, Og also curled up and went to sleep. Kean shrugged, returned his sword to its scabbard and tucked the grant under his arm. Tiggy carried Allie's satchel and they crept past the Goblin who continued snoozing to the music. Allie didn't stop playing until they had put considerable distance between themselves and the Goblin. Og woke and shook himself as Allie returned the cittern to the satchel and they resumed their journey.

Soon they climbed, pulling themselves up the side of a mountain.

Whoever built this path must be a giant and I hope we won't encounter any of those.

Allie didn't give voice to her worries; they had enough already.

Sometimes, Kean had to lift Og and the Leprechauns up onto step-like ledges and they in turn helped him climb up to them. They lit a firebrand when the path led them through a dark bat infested cave and emerged through a hole in a mountainside gully. Scattered bones and the cold remains of a cook fire told of a mountain inhabitant that had spent a day—or night. They had sore fingers, their arms and legs ached from the effort of climbing the steep mountainside. Og stopped on a ledge, his sides heaved. They flopped on the ground and drank from their water skins. Willy pulled out his cooking pot and they poured water for Og. The Grant drank his fill then trotted to the edge and rose on his hind legs to survey the forest below. His tail swished, he stamped his feet and tossed his head but he didn't scream. Instead, he pawed the stony ground with a tiny hoof, his brown eyes appealing. Curious, they moved to the edge to see what troubled him. A Campsite in a clearing far below drew their attention.

"Looks like an army." Kean pushed a branch aside.

"Yes. An army layin' wait for us at Raven's Bend, but how did they know we were comin'? Thanks be to the badgers for warnin' us." Tiggy nodded at those assembled below. "Whoever they are, they can't be too bright sendin' Hobsnotters as forward scouts."

"Is that what those things are that attacked us?" Allie turned away from the edge. "They didn't put up much of a fight."

Allie finally knew about Hobsnotters.

"Send one Hobsnotter to do a job an' he'll probably do it," Tiggy told them surveying the scene below them. "Send the whole mob and they can't resist attacking. They always attack from the safety of numbers."

"Good thing they did attack us," Kean sighed, "otherwise we might have walked straight into an ambush."

"Thank you, Og." Allie spoke aloud, kneeling and resting her forehead on his. "You truly are Og the Defender."

They washed and patched up the cuts and scratches; Og had the most. A hasty meal of bread and hard cheese slaked their hunger before they set off again. Og led them toward the top of the mountain range. Late in the afternoon, misty rain began to fall. They made camp under an overhanging rock on a bend in the rough trail they now followed.

Once again, they went without a campfire fearing they would betray their position to the enemy below. For the fourth night they ate bread and cold cheese, this time washed down with berry wine. They fed Og all the apples he could eat along with a bowl of the oats that Tiggy had bought at Glade Cloch. The meal over, they prepared their bedrolls for the night.

"Sleep Og, you've earned a good night's rest. Tiggy, Willy and I will take turns at keeping watch." Kean spread out the leather pack roll on the ground beside Allie's and pointed Og to lay on it. The Grant curled up and Kean covered him with his blanket.

Kean pulled his hood up, "I'll take first watch."

"Why do you suppose that Goblin keeps his boogers in a bag around his neck?" Allie asked the question that had played on her mind all afternoon.

"Treats." Willy's drowsy voice came from his blankets. "For his pet Hobsnotter."

Kean guffawed. "Really?"

"Mm." A snore issued from Willy's blankets.

17

<u>Whiteout</u>

They ate breakfast in the dim morning and set off up the mountain range. The misty rain turned to floating snowflakes and made the trail treacherous underfoot. This mingled with weariness from their ordeal of the day before, slowed progress. They reached the mountain top by mid-morning and appreciated the smoother terrain. Seeing a hulking being much taller than Kean, standing nearby, alarmed Allie and Kean. He surveyed them with blurry eyed indifference.

"Uurgh!" He dismissed them with a wave, turned and slouched into his cave.

"What is that?" Kean asked.

"It's a Tarragon Mountain Troll." Tiggy kept his voice low.

"I wonder why Og didn't scream?"

"Because he knows they won't hurt you if you leave them alone."

They saw two more trolls that day; the first excavated a larger entrance to a cave. Kean mused he must be an adolescent, evident by the livid red pimples on the doltish face he turned in their direction.

"No doubt, striking out to establish himself in the world."

The second ignored them as it peered at a last apple on a high branch; it shook the tree and mumbled to itself. Beside it on the ground, brim full with apples, sat a basket so big Kean could have curled up in it.

That night they made camp on the leeward side of some rocks beside the road. They didn't make a fire but huddled together to keep warm. Early in the morning, a high-pitched scream awoke them.

"Og?" Allie rubbed her eyes.

"It weren't Og." Tiggy jumped to his feet along with Og, who had been sharing his blanket, "but t'was surely being a Grant that screamed."

"It came from down that way." Willy had been sitting watch and pointed down the northern slope.

"We better move quickly." Kean rolled his pack and hefted it over his shoulder. "Let's go, we can eat later."

They needed no urging—they packed up and moved in a north-easterly direction along the top of the mountain. In the dim morning, they could see glows and points of light—campfires on the side of the mountain. Further along, they passed a wooden sign pointing to a narrow road down towards Dorcha Wood. The writing had long since faded.

The snow fell heavier and the mountaintops blanked out. The wind increased and the temperature plunged. They took a break in a sheltered outcrop and Kean observed rather optimistically, if those down the side of the mountain pursued them, they'd have trouble.

"Trekking up the mountain side in this weather will be hard enough, and they won't be able to see our tracks even if they do make it."

"Meanwhile we'll freeze to death," Allie shivered and pulled the fur lined hood of her cloak closer around her ears. The snow pelted ever harder, growing deeper, it threatened to bury Og.

Tiggy took out a sheepskin horse blanket and pulled it over Og's head, the Grant reared to survey the trail behind them.

"Stand still! If ye don't wear t'is ye'll freeze!"

Og screamed in Tiggy's ear.

"Shut it ya stupid mule!" He growled.

Another scream sounded from back along the trail and they scrambled to their feet with weapons ready.

"Come out an' be showin' yerself!" Tiggy shouted into the wind.

Out of the white mist, another Grant loped through the snow, black like Og but with a white blaze on its face and wearing a sheepskin rug similar to the one Tiggy had put on Og. The Grant led six people on horses; one carried a red and gold banner. They wore robes of black with fur lined hoods and carried spears and heavy bows.

Kean stepped forward his hand on the pommel of his sword. "Who are you and what do you want from us?"

They came to a halt; their horses tossed their heads and snorted at the appearance of three Leprechauns and a strange human.

"I am Aveline of Orghlaith," the girl lowered her hood and revealed pointed ears poking through her fair hair, "With me are Seamus, Niall, Garbhan, Luisech and Lorcan, all of Orghlaith. Our Grant's name is Ki the Courageous. What is your business on Tarragon Mountain?"

"We are travelling to the Mountains of Fuar Lae." Kean's fingers relaxed a little. "We've had to take a different route to that we had planned."

"So it is you the Clurichauns and Goblins are chasing." Lorcan jerked his head in the direction of the Goblins. "We've stopped them for you, and the Trolls are now watching the road should they return."

"You will either have to go back the way you've come or travel on with us to Orghlaith," Aveline's eyes moved over them, "but first I will have you tell us who you are."

Tiggy spoke up, "We are Tiggy, Willy, Kean O'Hara and his sister, Allie."

"Sister?" Aveline raised an eyebrow. Allie noticed Lorcan looking at Og, pondering why a Grant accompanied ordinary travellers.

"Adopted." Kean lifted his chin, "it was kind of the Leprechauns to take me in."

"Why are you travelling to Fuar Lae?"

"To visit my family." Kean lied a little too easily and Allie could see he failed miserably.

"Your family? You said you were adopted."

"It's complicated."

Aveline narrowed her eyes. "Besides, as far as I know there are no big people in the mountains of Fuar Lae." An embarrassed silence trickled in. "In fact the only people I know of there are the Dwarfs and refugees from Rois who live in a village called New Rois."

"I will tell you who we are." Allie spoke before Kean began again, "but first I must know if you are allies of Idé Mae Etain, the usurper queen of Rois or any from the villages of Kipper Hollow or An Dara Choróin."

"We are not allied with anyone." Aveline open her hand to the mountains around them. "We live side by side with the Tarragon Trolls. It's strange for the Goblins to chase you, I've never known Goblins to pick a fight with anyone except other Goblins."

"I need your trust." Allie tried not to sound nervous. "You've seen what we face if we return to Dorcha Wood."

"You can trust us, though you have scant choice as I see it," Aveline glanced at the sky. "This weather is not going to ease for many days which is why we are in such a hurry to get back to Orghlaith. Tell us quickly so we can be on our way, for we must soon be moving."

"I am Alastríona of Rois, my companions are my adoptive brother Kean O'Hara of County Breagha, Tighearnan son of Tighearnan, of Turloch, Ullian son of Ullian, also of Turloch and Og the Defender of the Dorcha Grants. We are travelling to Fuar Lae to my grandfather, King Etain who has sent for me."

"Well, Your Highness," Aveline and her fellow riders bowed their heads though they didn't dismount, "you can ride up here with me, the rest of you double up with one of the others and we'll make for Orghlaith."

They rode double with Aveline's riders on their sure-footed mountain ponies, Og and Ki led them along the crest of the mountain. The wind rose to screaming pitch and slowed their progress but the Grants instinctively followed the trail.

After hours of travelling through the blizzard, Allie could make out the dark figures of enormous stone statues along the sides of the road, statues of people—some on horses. Several were of dragons.

Red and gold the hue of her hair,

her beauty and her youth be fair·

The air shall be white, cold mountain her flight,

Golden Dragon her burden to share·

19

The City of the Golden Dragon

Many tiresome hours later, Orghlaith loomed big and dark before them. Snow encrusted the manes, tails, and nostrils of the brave little grants, Og and Ki, as they halted in front of the enormous wooden gates. A voice barely audible in the screaming wind called from above and one side of the double gate rumbled opened. Ahead, lay a grey stone castle, its great towers and battlements just visible through the white. Stone buildings lined the road leading to the castle, an inn, a blacksmith, potters and tinkers. Orghlaith was a prosperous city. They rode on past the stalls and entered the castle by a side door. Grooms stepped forward to take their horses. Og and Ki stayed with the humans.

Aveline removed her cloak. Underneath she wore black breeches and a tunic covered by an armoured vest of leather with brass scales sewn all over and a golden dragon with a red background on the breastplate. The others removed their cloaks as well and for the first time, Allie saw there were two girls in the troop. The men, Seamus, Niall, Garbhan and Lorcan like the girls were tall with fair hair and pointed ears. These were not people like the O'Haras. They were Elves.

Aveline showed them to a room with a long table and a blazing fire crackling in the hearth. Hanging overhead and standing along the walls, many candles burned in iron candelabras. Portraits hung around the room, of Elves and a number of Dragons. Such was the skill of the artist, the eyes of the subjects seemed to watch the visitors, silently observing from the past.

"Wait here please, make yourselves comfortable."

Allie smiled as Kean stepped sideways, the better to view Aveline as she strode out the door. They waited, warming themselves by the fire. Tiggy and Willy closed their eyes and relaxed, weary from the gruelling ride, Ki and Og curled up on the rug and slept, steam rose from their damp coats. Presently, a group of servants entered carrying a steaming pot, a platter of bread, bowls and a stone flagon of wine. They savoured the stew and bread after a whole day with nothing to eat. As they mopped up the last of the stew, the door opened and Aveline returned with an elderly man and woman.

"Welcome Princess Alastríona of Rois to the Elven City of Orghlaith, the City of the Golden Dragons," said the man, "I am King Liam, and this is my Queen and wife Liadan."

Allie and her fellow travellers rose to their feet and bowed. "Thank you for your hospitality."

"The prophecy of Taliesin the Bard told of a Leprechaun Princess who would return in a blizzard high in the mountains." The Queen gazed over their heads as she spoke. She wore her long grey hair braided with threads of red and gold and beads knotted into the ends. She had on a simple gown of cream with red and yellow ribbon stitched around the hem. The Elves had slanted green eyes like the Fae. "It was foreseen the princess would be young and beautiful with hair of red and gold. I have waited many years knowing someday Taliesin's prophecy would bear out; his truth unassailable. Unity will once again return to the Mystical Realms." She lapsed into an ambiguous silence that left Allie dumbstruck.

So what am I to make of that?

"You must stay at least until the storm blows over," King Liam continued as though his wife hadn't spoken, "my servants will show you to your rooms where you can freshen up. If it is your wish you can join me in the parlour and we can become better acquainted."

After a hot bath and clean clothes, the travellers relaxed in the King's parlour, the fire crackled in the hearth warming the room against the howling wind outside. His servants brought wine, cheese, and bread on simple wooden platters. When everyone had a drink in their hand, the servants stepped into the shadows. The strength of the Elf wine surprised Allie; it was much stronger than that served by the Faeries and the berry wine the O'Haras made.

The Elves proved less formal than the Faeries of Glade Cloch and Allie, Kean, Tiggy, and Willy talked with the King, his son Prince Sarrián—Aveline's father—and others of the Royal Court. When they had enough of the wine the King's servants brought tea, Allie spent hours chatting with the King. He shared his knowledge of the history of Dorcha Wood, Rois, and Tarragon Mountain.

Allie watched Kean from a distance as she listened to the king. Kean only had eyes for Aveline, turning on his Irish charm and listening raptly as she spoke.

The lands of Rois, undivided will be,

when united are precious metals, three·

Pink stone in gold, silver sword old,

and iron tool of toil be key·

20

<u>The Wisdom of Orla</u>

They slept late, the blizzard continued and Allie woke to the sound of the howling wind buffeting the castle. Unwilling as she was to leave the warm soft Elven bed, she steeled herself to rise and dress. A servant showed them to the King's dining room for breakfast. Kean made straight for Aveline who seemed pleased to see him. Allie thought of Nyvián whom she missed so, it hurt.

Will I ever see him again?

Following breakfast, the King and Queen approached Allie.

"Orla has agreed to meet with you Princess, if you will accept?" The king smiled. "He hasn't agreed to speak to anyone from outside of Orghlaith for many years. You would do well to listen to his wisdom."

Allie, on Kean's prompting, slung Alastor's satchel over her shoulder. She accompanied King Liam in his carriage to the home of the dragons, an enormous cave in the northern side of the mountain, at the edge of Orghlaith.

Their footsteps echoed on the immense stairway leading to an antechamber.

"I'll wait for you here." King Liam took a seat against the wall. "Gilroy will take you through to Orla's parlour."

An Elf dressed in black with red stitching, gold buckles and trims stepped forward, "This way please, Princess Alastríona."

He showed her into an enormous cavern, lit by a torch on the wall and two candles on a carved stone table. As Allie gazed around, her eyes adjusted to the darkness, the door closed with a resounding clunk and the room darkened. She trembled, Gilroy had left her alone in a room that would be

immense even for Kean, for a being of Allie's size it
overwhelmed; it appeared larger than the whole of Windy
Hill Farm.

Do dragons eat Leprechauns? Will I die in here? Is this a plot to prevent me returning my people to Rois?

Standing in the darkened room she could easily imagine all kinds of terrors. She cursed her trusting nature but strove to quell the rising tide of panic and muster what little courage she possessed. A sound reached her ears and she peered into the darkness. Torches spluttered to life and illuminated the room. Allie stood face to face with a magnificent golden dragon as tall as the O'Hara's farm house. His leathery black wings had golden scales on the foremost edge and bright red at the elbows. He lowered his gigantic horned head so Allie could gaze into his emerald eyes. She tried not to imagine him devouring her in one easy swallow.

"Good morning, Princess Alastríona, it is kind of you to meet with me." His voice rumbled. "I am Orla; please sit." He indicated the table between them.

"How do you do?" Allie squeaked and made an awkward curtsy, wishing that someone had taught her the correct way to greet such a being. The manners taught her by the O'Haras only involved humans. "Thank you for inviting me, I have many questions."

"It is an honour to have your presence here in Orghlaith," his voice vibrated in her chest, "The Dragons have high expectations of you."

Allie steeled herself. "I know so much is depending on me, but I don't know how I am to fulfil the task ahead. I'm not brave and I don't have an army, I find myself counting on the support of the Fae."

"Faeries are the Leprechaun's most crucial allies as well as having blood connections. Their fealty is of utmost importance to Rois. The Elves also have a historic connection with your people. There are some matters though, where you would do better to use diplomacy. There is more to bravery than knowing how to wage war, my child."

I can't imagine how.

"Many hundreds of years ago my kind were violent and greedy, they killed thousands of people, big and little. They believed themselves superior to all who walked the earth. Humans hunted us almost to extinction and we only had ourselves to blame. Those of us who now remain do not like war and oppression; we vowed never again."

Orla sat on his haunches, sighed and shuffled his wings then continued.

"The false queen, Idé Mae is an abomination that must be brought to justice along with her minions. Your people are not her only victims. She has drawn the Clurichauns and the Púcas into her evil. Their lives were miserable enough, but now they have the added sadness in their hearts, knowing the atrocities they committed—committed and can never take back. You must not brand them murderers. Idé Mae promised them a place—a better life but her treachery has all but destroyed them. Dorcha Wood floundered when Treasach the Truthful took the throne but Idé Mae has poisoned what little harmony remained."

"The Clurichauns and Púcas murdered a lot of my people, many of them children in their beds. Are you saying they shouldn't pay for what they did?"

"They've paid. For sixteen long years, they have paid every day. Yes." Sadness weighed on Orla's voice. "They suffer from their foul deeds, and such deeds must never, never be forgotten. Are you brave enough Alastríona, to forgive instead of punishing? It will take a brave heart indeed to forgive the terror committed on that dreadful night. But if you want everlasting peace in Dorcha Wood then forgive them you must." His great rumbling voice stressed these last four words. "Forgiveness is a magic all of its own, Princess."

Allie gazed at her hands and considered his words. Silence dominated the vast room.

Orla's voice rumbled into action. "Your great-great-grandfather, Treasach the Truthful, had an opportunity when he seized the throne to bring everlasting peace to Dorcha Wood, but he squandered it. His subjects were unwilling to allow the Clurichauns to live among them, for they do not make the best neighbours with their bad habits and poor manners. When the Clurichauns fled their ancestral home and needed refuge, the Leprechauns rejected them—that is how Kipper Hollow came to be.

"Instead of working to convince his subjects their charity would be worthy, Treasach chose the easy way and allowed the old prejudices to prevail. The Clurichauns are aimless; they have little interest in changing their lives for the better. Give them a chance, give them leadership and they might change. They must be included in your society, however uncomfortable that may be. By living alongside your people, with kindness and guidance, they will observe and learn. Allow a people to wallow in their failures without the will or incentive to change and they'll slip deeper and deeper into the mire such a miserable and inadequate existence brings. The Clurichauns have lived too long without a leader, pushed to the shadows of Dorcha Wood. Give them the same chances in life that Leprechauns regard as their birthright. If you are brave enough to do this, Alastríona, even if your people resent it, Dorcha Wood will reap the benefits in the years ahead."

"Why don't they have a leader?"

"There is a legend which tells of a king who over a century ago, ruled the Clurichauns, fell afoul of the Encantar, Dona Angrona the Mighty, an evil sorceress and he was believed slain as he was not seen thereafter."

Orla fell into contemplation for a moment.

"The legend said the sorceress cursed the Clurichauns forever to languish in an aimless and melancholy existence, never again to know a leader. Driven from their ancestral home of An Dara Choróin and exiled in their own lands. The legendary Máedóc banished Dona Angrona from Dorcha Wood, in a bloody battle that raged for days. He banished her, but we must assume she is still about because the curse she cast on the Clurichauns still binds them. There are occasional rumours of a shadowy figure that haunts the woods. I have investigated these reports to no avail."

What can I do to save the Clurichauns and how will my people like them living in their midst? Is there any truth to the legend of the Clurichaun king? Allie worried over Orlas revelations. *If the curse proves true, how will I lead the Clurichauns? For lead them I must if they would live among my people.* It would be brave indeed to ask such a sacrifice of the Leprechauns. Dare she ask it?

"I sense you have a kind and brave heart, Princess Alastríona. Be the heroine the folk of Dorcha Wood need, even though it is a need they may not understand."

"Orla?" she asked, "If I show you the two things my father left to me, I wonder if you can tell me what they are for, I mean—if they have a purpose?"

"Yes certainly." Orla smiled a paternal smile. She took the box and the cittern from the satchel and placed them on the table.

"The Cittern of Rois! A skilled luthier made it for a Leprechaun king many hundreds of years ago. I feared it had fallen into evil. For should evil control it, who knows what heinous deeds could it enact? Legends tell of the mysterious power it possesses. In the hands of Leprechauns, it is simply an instrument of sweet music, loved by all."

Allie was certain of a more sinister use for the cittern as she'd used it to lull the Goblins asleep as well as the hens and sheep back on the farm. "This box," she held it up and turned it over; it tinkled, "I cannot open it—there is no way in."

Orla's chuckle rumbled in his chest and echoed in the cavern.

"Your father like you was The Custodian. By Leprechaun magic, you succeeded him when he died and only The

Custodian can truly rule the kingdom of Rois, The Custodian has the power to make or break a King or Queen. Wait, it will open for you when all your living blood returns to Rois."

"But I don't understand, my grandfather reigns, not me."

"If you disapprove of his reign then you can withdraw your support and he'll no longer rule."

"How does that work?"

"The role of The Custodian passes down from generation to generation. When The Custodian's firstborn has a child, the firstborn becomes the Custodian. Alastor became The Custodian when you were born but because he died the title passed on to you. Angus the Erratic lost his crown when his son withdrew his fealty, denounced himself as Custodian and allowed Treasach the Truthful to take the throne. The role of Custodian passed to Treasach until his son's wife gave birth."

Allie bit her lip; magic was a complicated affair.

"Now Princess, I wonder if you would play the cittern for me, for it has been many long years since I have enjoyed the magic of its voice."

Allie spent the rest of the day and most of the night musing over Orla's council. She still worried a little about her role of Custodian.

All my living blood? What did he mean by that?

She wished she could now speak to Nyvián or Maghnus; even Patrick—certain they would offer her words of wisdom. She began forming a vague plan though without seeing what she faced to wrest control of Rois from Idé Mae, a vague plan it would remain.

One evening a tipsy Clurichaun,

sat backward upon his unicorn,

but it all went wrong and he felt a prong,

t'is luck only his bloomers were torn·

21

<u>Idé Mae's Ire</u>

Idé Mae wasn't a happy queen. The band of Clurichauns she had sent to capture Princess Alastríona, had returned beaten and bruised from an encounter with the Elves and Trolls of Tarragon Mountain.

"Why," she bellowed, "did you allow her to escape up the mountain?" She paced the throne room in a pother of bother. "My raven gave us ample warning of her approach, you could have met them head on but instead you cowards chose to stage an ambush! And whose idea was it to set the Hobsnotters to watch the path?" Her voice rose to a squawk, her eyes and throat bulged. "Didn't any of you know the badger you saw digging in the forest was a Faerie spy? Never trust a badger! Who ordered you to throw your lot in with the Goblins? Why, when the last time I was in An Dara Choróin they declared themselves my enemies?"

The small band of Clurichauns quivered at the foot of the stairs to the platform on which Idé Mae's throne stood. None dared speak.

"Well?" She puffed and swallowed air, her hands slipped off her hips. "Does any one of you have anything of use to say? It was a simple thing I asked, kill her servants and bring her to me! But no! You went off on a jaunt with the Goblins!" Her voice rose to shrieking pitch again.

"S—Sorry, Missus Queen," croaked a terrified Clurichaun, "The Goblins showed up and tol' us they wanted to 'elp—we t'ought—" He recoiled from her wrath.

"You thought! Not one of you is capable of thought!" Idé Mae inflated a little more.

Ultan the Evil entered the room, flicking his cat-o-nine tails, rather worn with many years of flaying—indeed, it was now a cat-o-seven tails. His eyes shifted around the room from Idé Mae to the Clurichauns and back again.

"Ultan! Take this band of lazy slobs up the River Síoga to the Elvenholt Bridge in the Caonach Valley. They will get one more chance to seize the Princess. If they should fail they will get much more than a tickle from your lash."

She watched the trembling Clurichauns scuttle out of the throne room with Ultan the Evil on their heels. She belched and returned to pacing.

Why is it so unsatisfying, being queen?

As a young girl, she'd envisaged life as Queen would be one spent receiving guests, hosting grand balls and lavish dinners—passing judgment on the disputes and crimes of her subjects, but nobody visited her palace, only Ultan the Evil and a few lowly Clurichauns. The Clurichauns had diminished in numbers too. She had imagined as queen, she'd be beautiful, but five years had passed since she'd had the mirrors in the palace removed; such was her horror at what she had become. The night before she had dreamed she was a child again playing on the farm with Prince Alastor and the O'Hara boys. Her father had called her to him, his dead eyes spilled tears of blood and he told her of his sadness that she was about to die. She'd woke with a squawk, her legs tangled in the lace curtains of her bed. She staggered, sweating to the kitchens in search of something to eat, for eating helped her forget when the nightmares invaded her sleep. She had found nothing she liked to eat in the larder, in fact, there was scant food there at all. Her shrieks and the crashes of pots fetched the servants from their beds, wide-eyed with fright. Her demands for food brought a fearful apology from the head cook and an explanation that there had been no food delivered that morning.

"What?"

"The farmers be no longer deliverin' to Rois."

Now, belching and blurting, she made one more circuit of her lonely throne room and remembered the inadequate lunch the cook cobbled together, her stomach rumbled for food of which there had always been plenty. She had sent a band of Púcas and Clurichauns to dispense justice for the farmers' impudence and grew anxious, they hadn't yet returned. Deep inside she always expected she would suffer the consequences of the brutality she'd had Ultan perpetrate in her name, for in spite of her callous nature, her humble father's lessons in humanity endured—ingrained in a remote corner of her cold heart.

As if she hadn't had enough aggravation for one day, she made her way to the palace treasury. She had not given up hope that one day the door would magically open and the gold inside would spill across her greedy feet. An iron cannon lay on the floor, the barrel partially melted from an unrelenting volley several months previous. The only product of that afternoon's work was a large hole in the outer wall of the palace from a ricocheting cannonball.

Fie Fíu as usual, lay on his massive warty back with his skinny leg hooked over the back of the now sagging and filthy divan. Her sudden appearance brought a *pa-roup* sound from the giant natterjack's bloated body. He opened one eye at her, and yawned, his capacious mouth snapped shut, his long tongue smacked and slurped. He fell back to sleep. "Fuffie! Wake up and talk to me," whined Idé Mae.

Fie Fíu snorted and almost rolled off the divan which had grown too narrow for him over the years.

"Wha? S'up my beauty?" he croaked and rubbed a wet hand over his eyes.

"The Clurichauns have disappointed me again, they didn't capture the Princess and they earned themselves a beating from the Trolls as well." She sat on the broken cannon.

"You can't depend on Clurichauns my beauty, they are much too lazy." Fie Fíu scratched his belly, it gurgle as a bubble of air rolled around inside.

"And there's no food."

This last piece of information gained the toad's full attention.

"What?" He almost sat up. "No food?"

"The farmers are refusing to deliver to Rois. It'll be those Faeries. They've never like me being their Queen."

"You? You are a Faerie Queen?"

"N—No! Of course not, but I am the Queen of all Dorcha Wood aren't I?"

"Um, yes indeed you are my beauty."

"I've sent a garrison to the Elven Bridge to try again to capture the Princess and I've sent another to remind the farmers along the river where their loyalties should lie, remind them who's in charge…"

A great croaking snore alerted Idé Mae that the toad had fallen asleep again. She filled the room with a sigh and her empty stomach emitted a querulous rumble. She marched to the pristine door of the treasury and kicked it, she shrieked in pain. Fie Fíu slept on and the shining door remained cool and unscathed; Idé Mae belched and limped back to the throne room.

****

At Turloch, north-west of Rois along the River Síoga, several hundred Leprechauns regrouped after driving off a desultory garrison of Clurichauns and returned to their preparations for when the Fae warriors from the Glade Cities would join them four days hence.

In the Mountains of Fuar Lae another army of one-hundred and twenty-seven Leprechauns prepared to march to Rois the following morning, having earlier that day elected their leader, a Hobgoblin called Manzukk.

The palace larder was empty and bare,

nary a crumb be found in there·

Not even a bean, for a hungry Queen·

Watch out! Prepare! Beware!

22

<u>Battle at Oakenhaven Pass</u>

As the storm abated a cold and weary pigeon arrived with a message from Maghnus addressed to King Liam;

'Hail Elven King Liam,

I feel I must warn you, we, the Fae of Glade Ceo, have observed a large and growing encampment of Goblins in the woods near Raven's Bend. I believe these Goblins are allied to a witch and are hostile. Regretfully, I can offer no additional information. We shall continue our surveillance and advise you of any changes.

'Have you seen or had contact with the Princess Alastríona of Rois? Our informants have been unable to locate

she and her party since they escaped a Hobsnotter attack six

days ago, we can only assume her Grant has led her to you.

'With the return of the Custodian Princess I feel the time

has come for our people to reunite and I pray the old alliances

still hold true.

My people convey their friendship to yours,

Maghnus of Glade Ceo.'

The news from Maghnus stirred fear in Allie's heart remembering her recent encounter with the Goblins, she wanted to hide forever here in the safety of the mountains with the Elves. Her fear increased when Elven riders returned later the same day with more grave tidings; another band of Goblins amassed at Oakenhaven Pass near the foot of Tarragon Mountain, the route Allie and her companions planned to travel.

With this new revelation from Maghnus, she dreaded the coming days.

Is the witch Maghnus spoke of, the one that cursed Ferghus? It must be. Is Idé Mae allied to the witch?

They spent many hours meeting with King Liam and Captain Glearán a tall, tough looking Elf with long silvery-grey hair, the highest-ranking officer of the Elven army. Several hours into the meeting an enormous, shaggy-haired troll called Ragnel joined them, clad in a tunic made of many rabbit skins. His bare feet astounded Allie—given the freezing conditions on the mountain. Ragnel didn't have much to say, he spoke in low grunts but he knew the mountain better than anyone did. They pored over maps of Dorcha Wood, Fada Woods north of the River Síoga and of the Tarragon Mountains. With plans in place, Liam sent his second and third messages in the past two days; to Maghnus of Glade Ceo and to King Finnán in the Mountains of Fuar Lae.

On the day they would leave, they rose early to hard packed and slippery snow—the air clear and freezing. Frozen daggers of ice hung from the trees, the walls, and the gargoyles on the castle. The weak morning sunlight refracted from the icicles, shooting flashes of light. Rainbow drops hung, glinting and fell from the lowest extremities.

"Orla has asked me to pass this on to you." King Liam gave Allie a small book with the Rose of Rois set in the golden cover. There was no key to unlock the cover. "He met with the other Dragons and they have resolved you should have it. He tells me that you and you alone, will be able to unlock the book."

Allie sighed.

What is it with these things I'm supposed to open with a power I don't possess? Orla has more faith in my ability than I do.

She stowed the book in the satchel with the other possessions she'd come to treasure, a link to a past of which she knew little.

Kean stood close to Aveline, face to face they held hands and whispered. Aveline's horse sniffed the scabbard on Kean's belt and snorted softly. Allie smiled happily and averted her gaze, she hoped he'd come back this way again soon. At the same time, she felt anxious; what if something happened to him?

'It would be my fault.'

Down the Elven Road led by a Grant, rode a garrison of two-hundred and thirty-five Elven riders, the archers at the rear, the pikemen and spearmen at the vanguard, followed by the swordsmen. They each carried a light but strong shield painted with a golden dragon on a red background. King Liam,

Prince Sarrián, and Captain Glearán led the Elves; behind them Aveline and her troop. In the middle of the procession, three ponies carried the little folk. At the flanks, eighty Mountain Trolls marched barefooted carrying heavy wooden clubs.

As they approached Oakenhaven Pass, the horses pranced and snorted, the smell of Goblin hung foul in the cold air. Glearán gave orders using hand signals; he waved his arms and directed the ranks into position. The Grant screamed unnecessarily; they knew what awaited them. As they emerged from the pass, Goblins charged from both side of the road. Though vastly outnumbered, the Elves did have an advantage of being mounted. At Captain Glearán's command the archers attacked from the rear flank, firing over the heads of the vanguard, raining the Goblins with iron tipped arrows, agonised screams told them the arrows had found their target. Only the Goblins at the front of the pack were safe from the volley, the archers loath to attack those closest to their front line.

Gleàrán roared, "Attack!" and the pikemen and spearmen charged into the Goblin pack with deadly effect followed by the swords, the Trolls roared and swung their clubs and the enemy's ranks diminished.

Captain Zuunk Mosskull of the Dorcha Goblins, set his sights on the little folk, two of whom fought alongside the Elves. He dashed through the melee, his villainous black eyes fixed on the cloaked and hooded figure taking no part in the fight. Zuunk needed redemption following his dishonour when she had escaped him the week before.

"Pruddy Prinker!" he chuckled and grabbed the pony's reins. "Ullow mah Pruddy Prinker!"

"Who're you callin' Pruddy Prinker, scum?" The figure on the pony lowered its hood. Alegutt Anvilarm, the dwarf and blacksmith of Orghlaith raised his broad axe and joined the battle.

23

<u>The Bogus Wayfarer</u>

Vraslá the Mountain Troll waggled her ears and sniffed the breeze. The smell of Goblins in the mountain mist, mingled with the smell of blood.

"Battle," she waved a meaty hand towards the mountain.

Allie exchanged a glance with Kean. Og too sniffed the air, he led them along a narrow path down the mountainside. They rounded a bend into a dense forest, the path wound through gnarled trees.

"How much further is it, Vraslá?" Allie asked.

Their destination the Elvenholt Bridge on the River Síoga, where they'd agreed to meet Tiggy, Willy, and the Elves. Kean had agonised whether to ride with the Elves or accompany his sister and Vraslá. Tiggy and Willy went with the Elves, the Dwarf Alegutt Anvilarm, disguised as Allie, would be enough to convince any Goblin spies that all three Leprechauns rode in the middle of the garrison.

"Day after t'morra, Prince."

Kean raised an eyebrow and Allie smiled. Vraslá didn't say much, but she spoke the language sufficiently for them to communicate. She'd agreed to accompany Allie and Kean down the mountain, taking a path known to the Trolls. She slumped along behind Og and sang the same haunting song, her voice rich and melodious. Allie didn't understand the song—the words were Trollish, but she knew the melody well enough to play it on the cittern when they made camp on the first night, Vraslá sang along and Og fell asleep by the fire.

The next morning, Og shocked them with a scream, echoed by Vraslá who also screamed—which in turned startled Og, so he screamed again. They greeted with relief, the sight of a red fox dashing into the trees. Og's mane stood on end and he spent the ensuing hours on his hind legs, anxious and alert. Vraslá too, scanned the undergrowth.

"Remember what Ferghus said about the red fox?" whispered Kean.

Allie nodded and scrutinised the surrounding woods.

Mid-afternoon, Og screamed again, this time it a young Faerie adventured along the Troll Path. He introduced himself as Creven and said he had seen enough of the mountain; he wished to return to Elvenholt Bridge. They introduced themselves by first names only and said they journeyed to Fuar Lae to visit friends. Og did not like the young Faerie. When they resumed their journey, the Grant insisted he follow rather than lead, he kept his eyes on the Faerie. Vraslá wasn't taken with Creven either, she turned her head to glance down at him every few steps, her fingers twitched on the handle of her club.

That night they camped in the trees beside the path, the young Faerie helped them build a fire. He looked on as Kean cooked a pheasant and offered to help stand guard. Allie watched surreptitiously, wary of this stranger though she had no reason other than Og didn't like him and she trusted Og's judgment far more than her own. Kean pulled out his sword, sat close to Creven, and began sharpening the blade. Creven shuddered and edged away. Kean appeared to not notice; he took out his axe and laid it on the ground between himself and the Faerie. Creven didn't move but stared at Allie with a hungry expression in his strange yellow eyes. Og paced, swishing his tail and Vraslá sat with her club across her lap. She wouldn't be singing tonight.

"What did you think of my home, Glade Cloch?" Creven asked Allie. "Did you meet Queen Madeléine and Prince Nyvián?"

"Yes, we did, we also met the Prince's father."

"Ah yes, Maghnus." He smiled and poked the fire with a stick. He carried no weapons and was familiar with the Faeries of Dorcha Wood.

Why is he this far from the Faerie mounds?

As she speculated about her instinctive mistrust of Creven her skin prickled with unease. He sat at arm's length from Kean and his iron axe.

Faeries don't like iron. Has Kean noticed?

She'd heard about shape-shifters, could this be what they dealt with here?

Kean bounced to his feet; the sharp movement made the young Faerie cower. Kean's eyes narrowed, he raised an eyebrow and moved away to fetch more wood for the fire. Og screamed as a branch above Kean cracked and fell. Kean slipped out of the way; he smiled at Creven and swung his axe into the branch. Allie glanced back at Creven in time to glimpse something ugly ripple across the Faerie's face.

"That was close," he laughed, his smooth, unfazed manner returned.

Og hissed.

When Creven curled up in his cloak some distance away, Allie sat by the fire with Kean and gazed in the Faerie's direction.

"What do you think?" she whispered.

"If he's a Faerie, I'm queen of the Trolls."

Allie's tinkle of Leprechaun laughter made Creven squirm in his bed.

Allie awoke to a scream from Og and a scuffle followed by a soft crack. A wail rent the predawn air, Vraslá grunted and cursed in Trollish. Kean and Allie came to their feet in time to see Creven vanish into the woods with Vraslá, club raised and in pursuit, smoke billowed from her. The Troll girl came to a halt at the edge of the tree line and slapped out the flames on the front of her tunic.

"Vraslá! What happen?" Kean halted beside her with his sword drawn.

"Sorry! Vraslá no good watch—sleepy, woke up and Faerie wassa try to steal bag with the song stick. He pelt hot at Vraslá, hit Vraslá with airfire."

Allie was relieved she still possessed her father's satchel and ran to check the contents remained intact. Kean and Og searched the surrounding woods for the Faerie.

"It's alright, Vraslá" Allie consoled her. "I'm sorry you were dragged in to this fight, when we get to the bottom of the mountain you will be free to go home."

Dejected, Vraslá sat by the fire and Allie patted her shoulder.

"No! Miss Prince, don't send gone away. Vraslá must help! You Queen, Trolls want."

With tears in her eyes, Allie hugged the Troll girl. "If you want you can travel to Rois with me, I'm honoured to have you as a guide and as my friend."

Allie and Vraslá hugged, they laughed and cried. They broke apart as Kean returned with Og. The pungent aroma of burning fur hung in the still morning air.

"What a mess." He shook his head at the girls. "Well, no sign of that Faerie fella. He vanished. You'd better let me carry that satchel, if he has another go he won't take it off me."

Og swished his tail, he was the happiest Allie had seen him since the previous afternoon.

24

Underground

Tiggy, Willy, and Alegutt fought ferociously midst the battle at Oakenhaven Pass, alongside the Elves and Trolls. The enemy were born fighters and the battle raged until late afternoon when the surviving Goblins fled down into Dorcha Wood. The Elves loaded the wounded into light wagons and hurried up the mountain to Orghlaith. They had lost twenty-seven men and another thirty wounded, the Trolls had no casualties. Aveline and her riders wanted to pursue the Goblins but Captain Glearán ordered them to stand down.

"Those were but a few of the Goblins camped at Raven's Bend, you could ride into a trap. We'll camp here for tonight and rest before we move down to the Elvenholt Bridge tomorrow."

Before first light the following morning, several miles from Elvenholt Bridge where the Troll Path joined the Elven Road, a scout returned to the garrison with news; a heavily armed band of Goblins moved east along the River Síoga.

"The only place they could be going, in that direction, is Fuar Lae or more likely, they plan to block the bridge." The scout held his winded horse's head as it snorted and pranced. "The encampment at Raven's Bend is empty and the Goblins there have moved towards Rois or Kipper Hollow—we can't be too sure."

Glearán ordered Alegutt to go with Tiggy and Willy to meet Allie's party. "They won't have reached the bridge yet, intercept them along the Troll Path and accompany them across the river and on to New Rois in the mountains of Fuar

Lae. We'll move downriver and chase the Goblins back from whence they came."

****

Having helped Vraslá translate the song she loved to sing, Kean and Allie now took part, Vraslá sang her part in Trollish while Kean and Allie hummed along, then they sang their part while Vraslá hummed.

> *Here is my home, on mountain high,*
> *The summers green and winter white.*
> *The woods below are old and dark,*
> *Through ages, bloom here in my heart.*

> *The earth is brown the sky is blue,*
> *The seasons pass, the world renews.*
> *Throughout this land, my people roam,*
> *Oh mother Ireland, my sweet, sweet home.*

Og swished his tail and trotted ahead, he periodically reared and surveyed the surrounded woods. Late morning, he squeaked and bounced off down the track ahead of them, kicking his heels in the air.

"What's got into Og?" asked Kean.

Tiggy, Willy, and Alegutt came riding around the bend, waving and grinning.

Late that afternoon they approached Elvenholt Bridge, a stone structure over the River Síoga, built by the Elves many hundreds of years before. The underbrush near the bridge rustled and erupted, Og screamed and Vraslá shrieked. The Grant charged headlong off the road—down the hillside, along the edge of the River Síoga with an athletic young troll and the rest of the party in pursuit. They deemed it unwise to clash with the dozens of Clurichauns that gave chase, brandishing axes and hammers. Og leaped off the river bank into thick water weeds and the rest of the party followed. The stunned Clurichauns balked and skidded to a confused halt, while the group in the rear slammed into them.

Allie realised too late, Og had led them into a peat bog. Down, down they sank, fighting to keep their heads above the quagmire dragging them in, Alegutt cursed and the ponies squealed. Allie fought to move her legs and arms as the peat tightened around her. Kean attempted to grab her arm but couldn't reach. Og had been their faithful guide throughout the journey never once faltering until now, Allie knew that she was going under and would surely drown. She saw Kean's head disappear beneath the brown mass and felt her own face slip into the rancid bog. Unable to fight it, unable to breathe, Allie was drowning. Cold air enveloped her legs; she fell through and landed in damp sand—alive!

Kean, Tiggy, Willy and Alegutt—ponies and all, fell around her. Vraslá flopped in the sand, bewildered. Og, the only one unsurprised, was already on his feet, swishing his tail and ready to move. They were underground in a dimly lit cave; a little stream of water trickled past their feet and wound its way ahead into the darkness. The whole cavern glittered and sparkled with dim, shimmering light.

"Did you know this was here, Og?" Kean asked, but Og already trotted off; he knew exactly where to go.

"Of course he did!" A chilling voice brought a scream from both Og and Vraslá. Creven stood on a boulder ahead of them, his laughter echoed in the underground cavern. "You've come far enough girly, your journey is done! I'll not allow you to destroy my life's work! You were right; I'm no Faerie. I am

Dona Angrona the Mighty! The most powerful sorceress alive! I am now within reach of my destiny, to rule Dorcha Wood for all time. I have but to destroy you and remove all hope for the Leprechauns. The little folk's alliance with the big folk will hinder me no more! That sword shall harm me not! I've no need of the precious key you carry, Custodian! Everyone will revere and exalt my power! There can be none who oppose me!"

He transformed from the dashing young Faerie into a black cloaked witch, an ugly green-skinned spectre, taller than Allie by a head and shoulder. Red cat eyes glowed in the gloom, and her long black hair hung like curling curtains of snakes around her hunched shoulders, down her back and around her legs and ankles. "Your return to Rois doesn't fit my plan, Princess, therefore you must die!"

Kean drew his sword and ran at her. The witch flinched, fear flashed across her face, she raised her long green hands and closed her eyes. The ceiling cracked, rumbled, Kean scrambled dragging Og with him as rocks and boulders rained, he dived and landed clear, showering pebbles. Vraslá and the ponies screeched in fright. As the rumble died, they heard the witch's laughter fading. The cave turned pitch dark.

"Is everyone alright?" Allie asked, her heart thudded, panic paralysed her. She rose and groped her way around but desisted after she'd stood on Tiggy's foot and Kean's fingers in turn. Everyone was safe.

"What is this place anyway?" She could see no way out of this cold, damp darkness. Their loved ones would never know to where they had disappeared.

Tiggy's voice echoed in the dark. "I believe we are in the Crystal Caves. I never knew where the entrance was. The old stories tell of an underground world beneath the River Síoga that runs fer miles all the way to Rois. I didn't think the stories were anythin' more than myth."

"Pity old Groaner destroyed it." Kean muttered. "We could've used it as a short cut."

"I'm so sorry, everyone," Warm tears fell on Allie's cheeks. "It's because of me we're here and I don't see how we can escape."

Kean fumbled around in the dark, found his sister, and put his arm around her. Time stood still in the dark, Allie's mind in turmoil as she tried to think how they would escape. They heard a clinking sound and saw a spark. Willy used his flint and axe, trying to light a fire. Over and over he tried.

"It's no use, my kindlin' is wet." Silence overwhelmed the moment.

Ahead, Allie saw another spark in the darkness—another and again. A silvery light at first small, flickered to life and grew brighter—hanging in mid-air before them. They shielded their eyes. Six or perhaps eight Leprechaun sized creatures moved into view, splashing in water and picking their way through a gap in the rubble that had been the roof of the cave. Allie blinked her eyes and tried to see if they were friend or foe.

"Hello?" She trembled, fearful these beings may be allies of the witch.

"Hello! Hello!" Singsong voices mocked her—they giggled themselves breathless. "Hello, hello, hello."

"Who are you?"

"Hoo-wa—Hoo-wa—Hoo-wa!" The giggling erupted again.

"I don't think they understand what you're saying," Kean whispered.

They came into view. They had human heads and arms but from the waist down they were—fish? No. They had brown fur and large flippers like those of a seal, but when they crawled out of the water, the flippers transformed into legs and the fur became smooth brown skin. They had big friendly dark eyes in their dainty faces and shining copper brown hair. Some wore it long, others short. Their clothing material rippled like soft leather and they each wore different colours but mostly silvery-green, and the males wore a different style to the females.

"What—who are you?" Allie repeated.

"Hoo-wa—Hoo-wa—Hoo-wa!" They giggled and leaned on each other for support, weakened by their mirth.

A larger of these creatures splashed into view. An older version of the others, he had a more serious nature.

"Hello," he said, and Allie was sure he knew what '*hello*' meant. "I'm Tadg. I must say we haven't had a visit from

Leprechauns for many long years." His large brown eyes widened when he saw Kean. "A blunt-eared Elf! We've never seen one of your kind down here."

Kean laughed helplessly at his description, and the adolescent creatures laughed gratuitously with him, tears rolling unchecked down their cheeks.

"But you have Faerie blood in your veins," he informed Allie. "Yes, I know this. Faerie blood." He peered around and his eyes fixed on Willy. "I can see a shade of Hobsnotter in you, sir, yes a quarter-blood Hobsnotter I think."

That observation rendered Kean weak and unable to stand, much to Willy's disgust. Kean's new friends put their arms around his shoulders and giggled with him while his companions looked on dismayed.

Tadg took a step backwards as Vraslá stood up, his mouth hung open before the power of speech returned, "A giant!" Delight spread across his face.

"Troll." Vraslá corrected him.

The sight of Alegutt made Tadg writhe with enchantment. "And a dwarf!" His large brown eyes grew teary. "Dwarfs bring good luck."

Alegutt's scowling countenance should cause the most optimistic being to cower, though Tadg rejoiced his good fortune.

"Please, sir." Allie found her voice at last. "Can you tell me what—um who you are?"

"Ah yes, got a little off track for a moment," sniffed Tadg, "forgive me, I don't often get much intelligent conversation down here."

Allie raised an eyebrow at Kean who shook with laughter.

"We are Selkies. Our kind have lived in the Crystal Caves forever. These are our young folk," he motioned to the gigglers. "Gerry, Penny, Neasa and Mahon and um—well that's them."

Allie introduced herself and her companions, feeling confident she could trust the Selkies.

"Come," Tadg turned and beckoned them to follow. "I'll take you to our lodge; it is much more comfortable than here."

He examined the wreckage of what was once a beautiful entrance cave and intoned, "Dona Angrona eats far too much red meat. Yes, red meat I think. Causes aggression you know?"

This time Allie joined in the hilarity.

25

The Imprisonment of Idé Mae

Idé Mae was displeased, to say the least. She fidgeted on her throne having listened to a report from the raggedy band of Clurichauns she had sent to Elvenholt Bridge on the River Síoga.

"I told you I wanted the Princess alive!" She squawked her frustration, she rose, belched and descended the stairs to pace the room.

"We were tryin' 'ard to catch 'er your Royal Queeness, but 'twas too lete!" quavered the leader of the Clurichauns, "they drewned themselves in a bog. As we be watching they was swallered—they sunk an' drewned."

"Ultan!" Idé Mae screeched. "Where's Ultan when I need him?" She glared at the Clurichauns. "Get out! Out I say!"

A harsh cackle from behind gave her gooseflesh; she swallowed a gulp of air. She spun around and looked up into the terrifying visage of Dona Angrona—baleful red eyes shadowed with purple in a green-skinned face. The pointed, yellow teeth bared and Idé Mae caught a whiff of her acrid breath.

"The Princess is no longer your problem for I have killed her!" The witch's long, knobby fingers closed around Idé Mae's throat. "Your conquest of Rois has served my purposes for some years, but now I no longer have need of you. You can join King Toad in the cage I think. Yes, I'll keep you for my future amusement."

She dragged Idé Mae, belching along the hall—down the stairs, out into the cold twilight and threw her into a heavy iron cage in the middle of the Palace of Rois' forecourt. Already in the cage sat a woebegone Fie Fíu, wide awake with, a belly full of air, and his hands clutching the bars as though his life depended on it.

"I'm sorry, Fuffie," Idé Mae cried. "The princess is dead."

Fie Fíu's stomach deflated loudly.

There once was a Leprechaun Queen,

lacking in food and growing quite lean,

The witch bared her fangs and the jail door clanged,

Captivity; Queen and Toad, unforeseen·

26

Rise

On the Elven Road before dawn, at the foot of Tarragon Mountain, an Elf scout arrived on his winded horse to report hundreds of Goblins approaching west; they would be upon them within minutes.

King Liam wheeled his horse to face his troops.

"Hark friends, hark! The Elves and Trolls of Tarragon Mountain have enjoyed peace for many generations!" His voice carried in the cold morning air. "Peace comes at a cost and it is time for us, the folk of the mountains, to pay our part of that cost. Our Leprechaun brothers and sisters have not been so fortunate, driven from their ancestral home to live in exile. The Elves and Trolls will no longer stand by and leave them to their fate! Too long, we have allowed the forces of evil to gather strength; today must be the day we say no more! Let this day be a new beginning! This day shall rise above the myths and mores of Dorcha Wood. Stand with me! Elves! Trolls! Let us fight side by side! For the Princess Alastríona! For King Finnán! For Leprechauns! For the Magical Realms! Let us fight!"

The Trolls and Elves roared, brandishing clubs, spears, swords and fists.

"Let us ride! Let us fight!" King Liam wheeled his horse and led the charge.

"Ride!" The voices behind him roared. "Fight!

They thundered towards the enemy, the rising sun behind them their glaring ally. The archers fired their arrows high overhead, their deadly shower rained on the sun-blinded Goblins. The spears and pikes charged into the pack, Goblins fell and scattered into the surrounding woods, the Elves and

Trolls chased them back from the river into the depths of Dorcha Wood.

The Elves halted on a small ridge overlooking Daione's Path, below them the Goblins they'd chased re-joined their fellows. King Liam stared, alarmed by the scene before him. A Goblin army numbering in the many hundreds gathered in a clearing and small but vicious group of Ogres stood to one side.

"We haven't seen Ogres in Dorcha Wood for fifty years." Captain Glearán pulled the reins tight on his prancing horse. "We can't pass this way to Rois. We'll have to go back and cross at the Elvenholt Bridge."

"That will add a day to the journey." Garbhan pulled his gaze from the creatures below. "I fear we may be too late. Those Goblins will arrive in Rois when the Fae and Leprechauns are already exhausted from fighting the Púcas and Clurichauns. The walls around the Palace weren't built to withstand a prolonged attack."

"There's a narrow path that runs along the northern bank of the River Síoga, I rode it in my youth." King Liam turned his mount, "We'll need to ride single file but it will be much quicker than the Caonach Road."

"Your highness, may I suggest you, the Prince and Aveline ride to New Rois and accompany King Finnán back to Rois?" Captain Glearán fell in beside him. "Take Luisech and Lorcan with you. If the fighting takes longer than I anticipate, I'll send a message to you. We must do everything we can to see King Finnan is kept safe. The Goblins may be watching the Caonach Road hoping to ambush the King's party as they pass."

****

Out of Glade Ceo, flew a swift army of Faeries with bows, long swords and silver shields, their chain maille glittering in the morning sun. In the ranks flew one who had more reason than any to fight; Ferghus sought revenge for his lost years.

211

In Glade Cloch Queen Madeléine delayed the departure of Nyvián's company by fussing over her nephew, she inspected the ranks and delivered a rousing speech. As the Glade Cloch army flew into the air over Dorcha Wood, Moyna's comforting arm around her shoulders gave Madeléine strength.

27

<u>The Selkies</u>

Tadg sent his eldest son, Ronán, to spy on Dona Angrona and report back. He sped off along the stream like a shadowy fish, out of sight in seconds.

"You'll be hungry." Tadg led them to the Selkie's village. They lived in cavities carved out of the rock walls of a large cavern, a widening of the subterranean conduit of the Crystal Caves. The hum of voices filled the air as the men and women chatted and worked side by side over a series of cooking pots and spits. "We don't often have visitors from the over-world, when we do they're usually not friendly folk. Just prospectors searching for treasure, of which we have none."

Allie fell in love with the Selkies. Their innocent view of the world at first disturbed her but there abided a quiet wisdom she found reassuring. Her own terror of Dona Angrona faded in their presence.

As they ate and drank with the Selkies, they discovered these people had scant regard for the Kings and Queens of Dorcha Wood and the surrounding mountains. Individuals and their achievements held their interest. They greeted with innocent incomprehension, the revelation of a wider world beyond Dorcha Wood—beyond the mountains. They had no interest in riches and from a quiet comment by Alegutt, Allie noticed the glitter of precious stones, gold and silver in the walls. The Selkies held no fear and little respect for Dona Angrona. Tadg related an incident years before when the witch visited them in the Crystal Caves seeking their allegiance, or perhaps Allie thought, to ascertain the possibility of taking control of this rich and remarkable subterranean world.

"She has no sense of humour," he lamented, "became most annoyed when young Ronán tied her hair to her bootlaces while she sat at the table. She didn't visit us for many years following that incident."

He looked around at his guests, bewildered by Dona Angrona's inexplicable rudeness. The adolescent Selkies roared with laughter at the retelling of this deed, a legend there in the underground. In the households Allie had visited in her childhood, children kept quiet and stayed out of the conversation—'*Seen but not heard.*' In the Selkie world, the children were the centre of attention. Never rude or unkind, but they were noisy as they romped around, laughing and playing.

Allie concluded the tendency for uncontrolled laughter was characteristic of the teenage Selkies; they continually pranked one another, the outcome always the same—the victim and the perpetrators together collapsed in paroxysms of laughter. The pre-teen Selkies were quiet and affectionate. One little girl climbed onto Allie's lap and piped words in Selkinese that she didn't understand.

"She says you look like a princess." Tadg translated and Allie smiled.

"Where did ye learn our language?" Tiggy inquired; a question Allie had longed to ask.

"The Princess' father—Alastor taught me," he said, matter-of-factly. When Allie had introduced herself he'd shown no sign that he was familiar with her family. "The West Fork of the Crystal Caves leads right to the Palace of Rois, into the cellar in fact. Alastor was a good, kind man—he had faerie blood too. We were friends since out early childhood. Yes, I miss my old Leprechaun friend. Ultan the Evil must die for his crimes," he spat, his faced darkened. "The false Queen Idé Mae thinks Ultan answers to her but she is wrong. They are all a means to an end for Dona Angrona.”

Nobody spoke for a moment, the teens at the other end of the room chatted and giggled over a game. Serenity returned to Tadg's face.

“Alastor used to play beautiful music on that wooden thing he had.”

“You mean this?” Allie opened her bag and pulled out the cittern. Allie played for the delighted Selkies; even the teens fell silent. Vraslá joined in and together, they sang her song.

Ronán returned as they neared the end of the feast. “Seems Dona Angrona has determined it's time for her next move,” he told them calmly, “she's taken control of Rois. Idé Mae is locked in a cage in the palace forecourt with a big ugly toad.”

28

<u>Through the Crystal Caves</u>

Allie accepted with gratitude, Tadg's generous offer of Ronán and his warriors.

"Now that I know we can enter the palace unseen, your men will be invaluable. I don't know how to thank you."

"You can thank us by coming to visit us once peace has returned. We love to have visitors from the over world." Tadg, flanked by a crowd of Selkie men and women waved and watched them out of sight. Ronán and a number of fierce, older Selkies—Lonán, Odrán, Ladg, Hadrán, Malag—and eighty other warriors accompanied them. They wore heavier clothing than the other Selkies, their leather and brass head gear had long sharp horns with colourful decorations. Their faces painted white with black around their eyes for ferocity. The spearmen carried long sharp spears and a brass reinforced shield slung over their shoulders. The bowmen wore a thick chain maille hauberk that cover them from head to knee with only face and hands showing, they each carried a heavy crossbow and quiver of iron tipped arrows. Some carried firebrands to light their way. A group of seven teens— including Penny, Neasa, Gerry, and Mahon, came along to help though evidently their admiration for their new hero, Kean, may have been the motive. The Selkies enjoyed this outing, rambling and splashing through the Crystal Caves. The underground stream that wound its way along their path grew wider and deeper with the cave. They had to climb over rocks and through narrow passages, Kean and the Selkies carried their four legged companions when they couldn't pass. Kean and Vraslá had to crawl in places when the ceiling of the cave arched low overhead.

Night and day didn't happen in the underworld, when they grew tired they stopped to eat and sleep. They awoke and continued until they came to a junction.

"That's the North Fork; it leads towards the Mountains of Fuar Lae. It comes out in Fada Woods." Ronán indicated a branch on the right; another underground stream flowed from it and joined the one they'd been following.

"Tiggy, can I ask you and Willy to go to Fuar Lae and bring my grandfather to Rois? Take Og, Alegutt, Vraslá, and the ponies with you."

"Yes, Princess. I'll do as ye bid but I fear I am breaking my promise to the King."

"I'll make it up to my grandfather." Allie smiled as Tiggy wrestled with contradicting orders. "I'm sure he'll understand."

"He asked me to bring ye to him…"

"Don't worry, I promise I'll keep her out of harm's way." Kean sat on a boulder surrounded by his young Selkie admirers. "We'll have Ronán and his men with us as well so I think we'll be safe enough."

Ronán sent the Selkie teens home, he wouldn't let them follow him into danger. Og led Tiggy and his companions away along the North fork to Fada Woods and New Rois; Allie and Kean followed the Selkie warriors through the Crystal Caves, a distant rumble sounded ahead and grew louder.

Hours later, the cave began to rise closer to the surface and the tunnel narrowed, they skirted a narrow ledge that overlooked the raging torrent below. The river narrowed and deepened; it wended its way ahead and thundered into a subterranean canyon.

"We are almost there," Ronán called over the noise.

"How did you get here so quickly when you followed Groaner?" Kean frowned.

Ronán smiled. "When we're not slowed by others we Selkie can swim as fast as a fish."

Allie noticed Lonán and Odrán peered with longing at the roaring torrent as though they'd wanted nothing more than to dive in and swim through the rapids.

The path became a winding stairs carved in the rock. Up it spiralled almost a full circle and back again until they came to a stone bridge that led across the underground canyon far below and then up a long stone stairway to a landing with a huge wooden door in a stone wall.

"This is it," Ronán patted the aged wood. "This door will take us into the cellar of the Palace. We need to unlock it."

"How did you get in yesterday?" Allie gazed at the door.

"I didn't come this way, I swam the rapids and into the lake."

"The lake?"

"Lake Aois, you have to swim through the rapids below then dive deep to come out in the lake. The River Síoga flows out of the lake right beside the Palace."

"How far is it?"

"Too far. We Selkies can make it because we are strong swimmers. No, we must find a way through this door." The flames of the firebrands reflected in Ronán's large brown eyes.

Allie examined the door; there was nothing to see—no catch or keyhole. Kean raised the torch, seeking the door's secret. He patted it, moving around the edges and onto the surrounding stones, listening for a change in the sound on the dark surface.

"Well, I guess it was never going to be easy." He sighed.

Allie tried, patting, rubbing, fingertips and palm—the door didn't move.

"Ah! To come this far only to be stopped by a door!" Not prone to fits of temper, Allie's driving impulse at that moment was to take the firebrand off Kean and set the door alight. As though reading her mind, Kean held the firebrand against the door—the flames flickered, dimmed and died.

"Wouldn't you know it?"

Allie stared at the floor, trying to think, one hand resting

on the door—Kean continued patting, rubbing and a half-

225

hearted punch, all to no avail. Ronán stepped closer and slapped it; the door flickered brightly for a second and faded.

Allie jumped back. "Do that again!" she gasped.

Ronán slapped the door again and nothing happened.

"Damn!" Allie turned away in frustration.

"Wait!" Kean caught her shoulder. "Put your hand back on the door Allie and Ronán you put yours on it too."

They hastened to heed his word. The door flickered and lit up; glaring silver light filled the landing.

"That figures," Kean grinned, "One Selkie and one Leprechaun is what it wanted."

Now a big, belligerent face stared out of the door with large rheumy eyes. Its cruel mouth quivered and it spoke with a rusty squawk:

"I grow with the green and sometimes red, alongside beauty but don't be misled.

I'm here to protect, my purpose is pain, from root to bud, I'm between the twain."

Allie and Kean stared. "What was that?"

The door repeated:

"I grow with the green and sometimes red, alongside beauty but don't be misled.

I'm here to protect, my purpose is pain, from root to bud, I'm between the twain."

"I think it's a riddle," Allie chewed her lip, "and we have to solve it. Let's see—'I grow with the green and sometimes red, alongside beauty'—that's a plant?" She glanced at Kean who stared at the ceiling, his lips moved.

"A rose! You're a rose!" he spoke to the door. It stared ahead unblinking, the lips pursed, its face showed no reaction.

Allie continued, "'I'm here to protect, my purpose is pain'—a spear?" The doors expression remained unchanged. "From root to bud I'm between the twain."

"A branch, No! A thorn. You're a thorn!"

The light flickered and died, the door clicked, the sound resonated in the stone stairwell.

"I won!" Kean grinned.

Ronán pushed the door from gentle to hard. Its hinges squealed with years of disuse. He cringed at the noise as he peeked through. They could hear distant sounds of shouts and fighting—the clash of metal on metal.

"Sounds like the battle has already begun." Kean whispered, "we're just in time."

He and the Selkies grinned in anticipation. Pushing the door wider, Kean, Ronán, Lonán, and Odrán slipped through. Ronán's warriors waited on the stairs for his order to advance.

"Allie, why don't you wait here while we take a look?"

"No! I'm coming with you. This fight is for me, so I should be there." Allie wished she felt as brave as she sounded.

29

The Palace of Rois

They assembled in the cellar, a cavernous room with a high ceiling—luckily for Kean. The Selkie warriors began to file through from the stone stairs below. Empty barrels and crates littered the room covered in dust; cobwebs hung everywhere. They left their packs; Allie kept the satchel with the cittern, the wooden box and Orla's golden covered book. They picked their way through the junk and climbed the stairs. Through another door they emerged into a large deserted kitchen, the Selkies filed in until the kitchen was full, a forest of long, sharp spears surrounded Allie; the Selkies stealth amazed her.

They crept across the room past a cold cast-iron stove; nobody had worked in here for several days. Ronán pushed the door open a crack, they stopped and listened; voices sounded from the other side.

"Who are they, these Faeries?" came the voice of Dona Angrona. "They don't wear the raiment of Glade Cloch."

A voice answered, "I believe they are from Glade Ceo, m'lady."

"Maghnus!" Dona Angrona growled. "When I was viceroy to the king at Glade Cloch he was a layabout Prince full of big ideas. I forced the King to banish him otherwise, Maghnus would be a toad not unlike the one we have out there in the cage. The King could not bear his beloved son so cursed. Loving parents are easily managed when their children are threatened." She cackled. "Even easier when they're weakened with poison."

"I 'ave sent a message to the Púcas to be sendin' more warriors my lady," came the voice again. "They should arrive any time now. An' I've 'ad word that the Goblins are on their way. Gnosag is bringin' the Ogre warriors."

"Good!" the witch sounded pleased, "they will be richly rewarded for their loyal service, as will you, Ultan. I want every available warrior out there fighting and defending the palace, it is secure but we must hold it. My enemies shan't keep me from my destiny any longer."

Allie's heart pounded; Ultan the Evil was so close she could almost smell him. She wished she had the courage to rush through the door and attack. Their fading footsteps echoed, a door clunked—they'd gone.

"Viceroy!" Kean breathed.

"Yes and now we know why Maghnus left Glade Cloch," whispered Allie.

Ronán gestured to his warriors to take the door at the opposite end of the kitchen and join the battle outside. With fierce grins of anticipation, they streamed out the door and disappeared into the cold morning light, through a postern into the village of Rois.

Allie, Kean, and Ronán tiptoed along a hallway and peeped around the corner into an enormous white marble room; its interior showed signs of a battle. A broken cannon lay prone beside a heavy log, pieces of rubble littered the floor. A large hole in the wall revealed pinkish morning sky over Dorcha Wood across the River Síoga. A few paces along from the hole, beneath large mullioned windows stood the filthiest divan Allie had ever seen. Its presence in this otherwise beautiful room mystified her.

They crept in to the throne room, Allie squealed as a fishy smelling net fell over them, ensnaring her and Kean. Ronán slipped out of the way in time. Allie found herself entangled and dragged with Kean by a gang of Clurichauns with red noses and bloodshot eyes, their harsh chatter echoed in the stone palace. The smell of alcohol wafted from them.

"Run, Ronán!" Kean shouted. "You can't beat all of them. Go!"

"I'll return!" Ronán shouted and darted back from whence they'd come.

They threw Kean and Allie, net and all, into a large iron cage in the castle forecourt. The door of the cage clanged and locked, the Clurichauns retreated, manifestly pleased with their catch. Kean borrowed Allie's short sword and began cutting the net.

"Dumb Clurichauns, they forgot to take our weapons. And now would be a good time for you to do your invisibility trick."

Allie struggled to free herself.

"Fuffie! It's the Princess!" came a voice from behind. Allie turned and saw a pudgy Leprechaun woman imprisoned in another cage with a gigantic toad. The toad hopped to her side and stared, bug-eyed.

"Princess! The witch told us you were dead!" The toad's warty hands clung to the bars. "You're alive! T'is be good news indeed!"

Allie gazed in horror. Idé Mae, though still plump appeared to have lost a lot of weight in a short period. Her dry scaly skin hung flaccid on her face and body. Her once red hair was sparse and almost white. Her scalp had bare patches; flakes of skin not trapped in her hair fell to her shoulders and across her toad like face.

"Good news? I thought you wanted me dead."

"Dead?" croaked Idé Mae, "No, we wanted you captured alive."

Kean got to his feet; his dark hair touched the top of the cage.

"What do you want with my sister?" he growled.

Idé Mae and the toad cringed. The toad's big wet tongue slapped around his face as he cleared his throat.

"I was the King of the Clurichauns," his voice shook with emotion. "Dona Angrona cursed me and made me what I am. Yes! Cursed me, to live forever—immortal—as a toad. Only the kiss of a true princess will break the curse. Yes indeed. I had hoped Idé Mae would be the one, but alas! She is nary a true princess and the curse is spreading to her. Yes! My beauty is becoming a toad like me.”

Allie felt sick at the thought of kissing this hideous creature.

“While the curse remains on Fuffie, the Clurichauns are doomed to an endless existence of despair and poverty. Since I took the throne the curse has strengthened,” Idé Mae eyes filled with tears. “I made a mistake. My stupidity and greed have caused untold harm to Dorcha Wood. I wish I could make amends, I wish I could undo what I've done.” She huddled, a small toad like body of abject wretchedness, sobbing into her pudgy hands. “I'd give anything to go back—”

The air crackled, the nightmarish spectre of Dona Angrona materialised and Fie Fíu inflated with a *foomph*. He rolled on his back against the bars; his bulging eyes peered over his groaning belly, his legs and arms flailed.

“How you escaped my rock fall I can't imagine. The Selkies will be punished, for this is no doubt their work.”

There to inspect her captives, Dona Angrona seemed reluctant to approach the cage. “This time you won't escape.”

A squeak of air escaped the toads distended stomach.

Dona Angrona ignored him.

"There will be a public execution as soon as I have finished with these troublesome Faeries. We will wait until your grandfather arrives, I think. I would hate to deprive him of such entertainment. Perhaps he can be part of it—yes! I would enjoy seeing the old Leprechaun execute his own grandchild."

Her long green fingers twitched on the wooden staff. Her menacing eyes lingered on Allie until Kean made a sharp move in the witch's direction. She flinched and staggered backward, her face twitched, her red eyes fixed on the sword. Her lip curled in a snarl and another flatulent burst exploded from Fie Fíu. The witch hissed, turned and stalked away.

"She's a bit twitchy isn't she?" Kean examined the blade. "I'm unsure if it's me or this sword."

Neither Allie nor Kean had taken seriously the information about the sword given them by Queen Madeléine, though now they had cause to wonder. Who had entrusted the sword to the Fae? What part had the big folk played in the history of the Faeries and Leprechauns?

An hour later, the battle beyond the palace gates grew noisier as though an increase in participants joined in. Weapons clashed; shouts and bangs echoed in the streets of Rois. Animal-like bellows of rage and pain issued—from what? Allie couldn't imagine. Then a different sound came from inside the palace, a sound of which Allie and Kean had grown fond. Chattering and giggling, the gang of Selkie teens emerged from the antechamber of the palace.

"Kean! Allie! Kean! Hello—hello!" They giggled and tottered across the forecourt and Penny produced a set of iron keys and unlocked the cage.

"Penny! Thank you!" Kean and Allie hugged the Selkies who dissolved into gales of laughter. Allie took the keys from Penny and unlocked the cage holding Idé Mae and Fie Fíu. Her intuition told her she had won their allegiance.

"I'm setting you free," she hoped her instinct wouldn't fail her. "What you do with your freedom will have a large bearing on what will be done with you afterwards. My grandfather, King Finnán's return to Rois is imminent."

"So mind your manners, Natterjack!" Kean tapped the toad between the eyes with the flat of his sword; Fie Fíu's belly inflated and flipped him onto his back again.

Penny's gang fell about laughing as the toad squeezed his stomach between his long hands and deflated it noisily. Allie worried the Selkie teens' hero worship of Kean could be dangerous here, given the battle in progress beyond the gates.

"Penny, take your friends and get back to the cellar, go quickly!" They scampered off, chortling and blowing raspberries.

As they left, Ronán appeared.

"Tiggy and Willy are bringing the King and his men, they should be here by tomorrow," he advised. "We've kicked out the Clurichuns and secured the palace, Tadg's command are now holding it in the name of the king. Only those on our side can enter."

"Allie, I want you to go in to the palace and stay there, and you must do as I say!" Kean looked fierce and Allie did as he commanded.

"You can take refuge inside the palace if you wish," Allie addressed Idé Mae and Fie Fíu, "but if you do anything against my people, I'll have you thrown out on the street to fend for yourselves."

****

Kean ran with Ronán through the gates and out to join the battle, at that moment, the Leprechauns from New Rois arrived led by Manzukk the Hobgoblin, fresh and eager to join the fight. The Fae and Leprechaun armies made a good show of hand to hand battle, attacking the Clurichauns and Púcas. Curiously, some of the older Faeries kept their eyes on the witch and Kean guessed they deflected her curses; Dona Angrona shrieked her frustration. The fiery red hair of the Leprechauns bobbed around in the dust and smoke, swinging axe and hammer. They drove back the Púcas and

Clurichauns—the latter's hearts weren't in the fight. Fighting alongside the Faeries and Leprechauns the black and white figures of badgers charged and clawed. Step by step, they drove the enemy out of the town square. A Púca rushed at Kean with sharp horns primed and murder in its baleful red eyes. Kean swung his sword and the Púca fell, bleeding at his feet.

As he sought his next opponent, his eyes fell on Maghnus battling a Púca, slashing with his sword, stepping nimbly out of the way as the Púca swung back, parrying, pushing and blocking. Back and forth they went, slashing again and again. The Púca charged, lunged for a death blow when, in a blur, he fell to the ground bleeding from a head wound.

****

"He nearly got you that time, Pa!" Nyvián grinned at Maghnus, blood dripped from his sword. "I arrived just in time. Please excuse our lateness; we were side-tracked by a battalion of Púcas headed this way. We sent them on their way back along the river." His mood darkened. "As soon as we dispatched the Púcas, we were attacked by Goblins. I lost two of my best fighters to them. When this is over, I think we should march on An Dara Choróin. That place has been allowed to fester too long." Nyvián frowned at the dead Púca on the ground before them. "I was almost too late getting here."

His father embraced him. "I'm glad to see you, son."

Nyvián gazed at the chaos that was the city of Rois. "I'm sure glad to see Kean—that means Allie is safe. News had reach my ears Dona Angrona had murdered them, but I wouldn't believe it."

"Nyvián!" Kean grinned when he saw him. "Come to join the fun? Grab a Púca."

"Where is Allie? Is she safe?"

"She's inside somewhere, staying out of trouble, I hope." Kean nodded towards the palace. "She'll be pleased to see you."

****

241

From the village of New Rois in the Mountains of Fuar Lae, a pigeon flew into the sky, its destination Windy Hill Farm in Breagha County; it carried a message for Patrick O'Hara. A second followed, wheeling in the direction of Orghlaith on Tarragon Mountain; a message addressed to Orla, the Golden Dragon.

A great ugly toad so dread,

erstwhile abandoned for dead·

Bring to pass what is just, love and sweet trust,

and the crown be restored to his head·

30

Ultan's disobedience

Allie surveyed the battle from an upstairs window when her eyes fell upon the one her mind refused to leave. Nyvián landed lightly in the castle forecourt.

"Nyvián!" She ran downstairs, through the entrance hall, down the steps. "Nyvián!"

Their arms entwined, Allie's heart leapt as his lips met hers, she felt the warmth of a silver aura light the air—

Or did I just imagine it?

"I thought you were dead, they told me the witch killed you. I knew it couldn't be true."

"She came awfully close—but—I'm so glad you're here!" Allie kissed him again.

"Ooh! Allie!" Smacking and kissing noises came from behind her followed by a chorus of Selkie laughter. Penny and her gang had returned.

"Friends of yours?" Nyvián kept one arm around Allie's shoulders.

"Nyvián meet Penny, Gerry, Neasa, Mahon."

Nyvián stepped forward to shake their hands but they ran off howling with laughter.

"What's so funny?" Nyvián touched his nose and looked down at his shirtfront.

"It's not you," Allie took his hand; "they're Selkie teenagers. Laughing is what they do best."

****

Dona Angrona had ordered Ultan the Evil to kill Kean O'Hara whose masterful hands held Argent Storm—Defender of the Dorcha Realm—Sword of the Big People. When held by the blood of Ó hEadhra, it poisoned her. Until they destroyed this sword and its owner, she could not inflict the cataclysmic wound needed to take unshakable control of Rois and the rest of Dorcha Wood. Dona Angrona could not approach the big dark-haired man—her bane—for the same reason she could not leave Dorcha Wood. She bemoaned every day, the magic pact between the Leprechauns and the Big Folk; Máedóc Ó hEadhra banished her from the woods, but the enigmatic Fae cast a spell that prevented her leaving.

What else would you expect from the Irish?

The reward she promised Ultan years ago remained unfulfilled. They thought their chance had come sixteen years before when Idé Mae arrived in the village of An Dara Choróin with the toad Fie Fíu. At that time, Dona Angrona served as Viceroy at Glade Cloch disguised as a young and ambitious Faerie called Ivor. Ivor the Conniver cursed the Royal family of the Faeries with a spell of discord that would, until broken, see the King and his son quarrel, morning and night—the King's son and daughter unable to agree on any one thing. The witch's efforts to destroy the sword failed when, as Ivor, she could not wrest the secret of its whereabouts from the old Chamberlain Martok. When a young and resentful Idé Mae came forward to mount all-out war on Rois, Ultan had feigned his allegiance. He trembled with excitement when he approached Dona Angrona with the news. Only the hand of a Leprechaun could mount an attack on Rois and only a Leprechaun could hold the city. Hold but never rule—only the Custodian had the power to decide who ruled the Kingdom of Rois. This quandary had enraged the witch for the past sixteen years.

"Destroy the sword and he who wields it," Dona Angrona instructed Ultan. "Then I will have the power to break the Leprechaun's Custodian spell."

****

Ultan didn't much care that the Goblin army failed to show as promised.

All the more for me.

The death of Kean O'Hara could wait for now—Ultan the Evil saw elsewhere, an easier opportunity to reap his supreme reward, the Prince of Glade Cloch and the Princess of Rois standing hand in hand facing the opposite direction.

Alas! Young lovers.

A cruel grin split his face. Ultan the Evil crept towards them, through the rose garden, sword at the ready. One swipe to break the hearts of both Rois and the Faerie kingdoms combined. He crept within striking distance. One step—his small, cold heart quickened. One step more…

****

Allie held Nyvián's hand as he told her of events since they'd last met. They both recoiled at a sudden scuffling behind them. They spun around in time to look into the sinister eyes of Ultan the Evil, his sword swinging—falling—

then he dropped like a loosed puppet between the rose bushes. Kean stood legs astride, over the twitching body, his handsome face dark with anger, blood dripped from the sword of the big people still held high in front of him. He sagged to his knees and the sword clanged to the ground.

"Allie!" Kean's voice shook. "I thought I'd be too late."

31

Late arrivals

Dorcha Wood trembled to a distant thundering, the sound of many voices chanting. Marching feet, booming drums, and crude horns trumpeted doom. Along Daione's Path, spears bristled skyward, six-hundred and ninety Goblins advanced on Rois. With them marched two score of Ogres carrying sharp spears, heavy clubs and battering-rams.

Maghnus ordered the Fae and Leprechauns, "Retreat! To the palace! Retreat!"

"Fall back to the palace!" Manzukk bawled to his troops and waved his broad cutlass towards the palace gates.

"Retreat!" The Selkies dragged their feet behind Ronán.

The Leprechauns, Faeries, and Selkies poured in through the gates and began barricading.

"Man the walls and parapets!" called Maghnus. "Prepare to defend the Princess!"

The remaining Púcas and Clurichauns fled through the streets of the deserted city. Their part in this war ended.

****

Allie took Idé Mae, Fie Fíu and the Selkie teens into the cellar.

"Barricade this door," Kean ordered, "don't open it until I knock like this." He tapped out a rhythm on the door.

Terrified, Allie hugged him around the waist. "Please take care!"

****

Nyvián and Maghnus stood shoulder to shoulder as Maghnus address the Fae.

"Fae of the Glade Cities! I need all the bowmen here in front of me. I'll also need curse deflectors as well!"

A crowd of battle-ready Fae warriors assembled.

"You will fly with Nyvián over the heads of the enemy and shoot as many as you can!" The Faeries cheered, ready to continue the fight. "Don't fly too low! Goblins are short-sighted but they can throw a spear high into the air! Curse killers! Keep the witch busy, she must not curse our fighters! Keep her away from the walls! Remember, you must stay well above range of the Goblins' spears, I don't want to lose any of you!"

His face pale and worried, Maghnus gazed at Nyvián. "Stay safe, my son."

****

Kean found Ronán on the wall, ready for battle.

"We're going to need more arrows, both light and heavy. Can the Selkies supply us?"

252

"You can count on the Selkies. I'll send four of my men back to the crystal caves and bring a new supply. I'll see to it more will be made as soon as possible. We're going to need food too, men can't fight on an empty stomachs and this could take a while."

Kean oversaw Dona Angrona's iron cages put to better use. A group of Leprechauns toiled to bolt the cages to the inside of the gates, reinforcing the heavy wood. They used every available cooking pot and bucket to carry water up on to the battlements, to the bulwarks in case the enemy chose to use fire. A second group of Leprechauns patched the gaping hole in the wall made by Idé Mae's cannon. They bolted the large wooden doors from the throne room to the wall to cover the hole.

The hour had arrived; the enemy bore down on them. Kean appreciated the skill of the Leprechauns as the gates took a pounding. A dozen Ogres rammed a long, heavy log against the gate, again and again; the booming terrorised those inside. The Selkie bowmen fired heavy arrows into the Ogres, some fell easily but others kept charging; arrows bristled from their tough green hide. When the Selkie's spearmen brought down their first Ogre, the fighters on the wall cheered and redoubled their efforts. Nyvián and his bowmen wreaked deadly havoc, firing from high into the Goblin pack though it took longer than hoped. Many Goblins fell, but hours later they still endured, numbers down but still a fearsome enemy. As Kean had predicted, the Goblins set fire to the walls, each time Kean and the Leprechauns doused the flames, refilling the buckets far below in the Crystal Cave stream. The Goblins threw hooks on long ropes over the walls and began climbing; the Leprechauns hacked the tough rope while the Selkies threw spears at the climbers. Whoops of glee marked each fallen enemy, the Leprechauns kept the hooks until their enemies had no more.

****

Allie gave up trying to barricade the cellar, Selkies and Leprechauns ran back and forth carrying buckets of water, and bundles of arrows and spears. Several Selkie women

254

passed, carrying baskets of fish and potatoes. Fie Fíu lay in the corner with a belly full of air. Allie and an unlikely volunteer, Idé Mae, set up a makeshift hospital in the throne room and to her dismay, the number of wounded grew. Nyvián flew in through the door carrying a wounded and bleeding Faerie, he placed him on the floor he zoomed back out without noticing Allie.

"Princess!" Allie turned to see Tadg bustling in the door. "You appear to need help, this is Dugán. He is the Selkie's medicine man. He speaks little of your language but he is a skilled healer." Dugán hefted a basket full of bandages, herbs and stone jars of medicine; he smiled at Allie and set to work.

There wafted a comforting smell of food from the kitchens. The Selkie teens carried food and drink to a long table in the palace antechamber, the fighters sat in twos and threes, bolted the food and ran to rejoin the fight.

The battle raged into the night and then abated to a few half-hearted sorties around midnight. Early in the morning, the exhausted fighters on the wall found themselves once again, battling an all-out attack. The Goblins roared and chanted as they charged the walls, the Selkies, Leprechauns, and Faeries rallied once more to fight on. Though exhausted, Allie couldn't sleep. She wandered out into the Palace forecourt during a lull in the fighting. She spotted Kean on top of the wall near the gate. Shouts of warning came from the Faeries as a lethal shower of spears hissed through the air, Kean rose to fire his arrow and a spear hit him in the chest. He fell like a rag doll, off the barricade down the outside of the wall. Icy panic pounded as Allie flew over the wall and dived to where her brother lay.

"Allie!" Kean gasped, "Go back inside! Now!"

Allie's relief at finding him alive turned to terror when she saw the spear in his chest. The Faerie maille vest hadn't prevent the spear piercing him, but it stopped it passing through his body. Nyvián and Maghnus alit beside her.

"Go!" shouted a white faced Nyvián, "We'll help him."

Allie sobbed. "Please help me get him inside!"

A grinning Goblin advanced on them, spear raised. Maghnus rose into the air and muttered words that Allie couldn't hear but a bright flash of white hot light hit the

Goblin, a shower of red sparks sprayed around him. The ugly creature fell in a smoking heap on the ground. Maghnus fell to the ground but recovered quickly. Nyvián and Allie, with the help of another Faerie, lifted Kean over the wall. Maghnus in deadly fury covered them, he fired spells at the Goblins and they ran screaming in pain. Maghnus collapsed to the ground, continual use of such powerful magic had exhausted him.

A bugle rang out from the east, from the north a horn resounded. An answering bugle echoed from the south and overhead came the screams of seven golden dragons, with them a horde of squeaking and chattering Ee-shees blown about by the draft from the dragon's wings. Captain Glearán led the Elves and Trolls as they charged into Rois from the east and with spears, swords, and arrows they attacked the surprised Goblins. From the south, Patrick, Rían and James O'Hara followed by sixty-three farmers and villagers from County Breagha poured over the bridge into Rois. From the Mountains of Fuar Lae, Alegutt Anvilarm led a legion of dwarfs, mounted on sturdy ponies and wielding broad axes. The dragons swooped over the heads of the terrified Goblins shooting long jets of flames, the Ee-shees flew screeching and firing sparks at the eyes of the intimidated Ogres who fled, chased by the Guardians of the Woods. The Elves, Trolls, Dwarfs, and Patrick's men chased the Goblins over the bridge and back into Dorcha Wood. Dona Angrona had disappeared.

****

258

Allie trailed the Ee-shees, pleading help for her brother and returned with a swarm of them.

"Allie!" Rían and Patrick both spoke at once. They knelt over Kean, with faces pale and eyes tearful.

"Father! Rían!" Tears streamed down her face. Kean still breathed but his eyes were closed and his face a deathly shade. The Ee-shees went to work and Allie felt herself drifting in and out of reality. Her eyes blurred with tears, raw terror coursed her veins—her shaking limbs numb and cold. Detached and distant, figures moved, whispering, arms closed around her. The sweet voices of the Ee-shees crooned and chanted, the spear in Kean's chest lit up and shimmered then dissolved into nothing. The air glowed with a warm golden light and calm returned. The Ee-shees fell to the ground, drained and Kean lay still, Dugán knelt to search for a pulse.

"Alive!" The medicine man's brown eyes glittered.

An hour later, Kean stood, defying Dugán's order to lie down. Maghnus had recovered too, tired but undefeated.

Long, long Ago in the times of Old,

for goodwill, the wrathful bell it tolled·

Evil spells were spoken and can only be broken,

when returns the Dragon of Gold·

32

<u>When All Your Living Blood Returns to Rois</u>

Hundreds of Clurichauns flooded back in to the city and surrendered, swearing allegiance to Rois, Dorcha Wood, and Tarragon Mountain. Allie waited with Patrick, Kean, and Rían, for Nyvián to return from helping Maghnus and Manzukk who directed the Fae, Leprechauns, Elves, Dwarfs, and Selkies to restore the streets of Rois to order. They removed the cages from the gates and took them well away—the Fae had tolerated the iron long enough. Allie puzzled over Orla's golden book when the call went out.

"Make way for the King! Make way for the King!"

260

A clatter of hooves echoed along the street, a small band of Leprechauns on galloping ponies followed by King Liam, Prince Sarrián, Aveline, and Luisech, bearing the flags of Orghlaith and Rois. Behind them Tiggy and Willy drove an ornate wooden coach pulled by six chestnut ponies. Og and Ki galloped beside them and Vraslá, jogged behind. Hooves clattered as they slowed at the gates and came to a halt in the palace forecourt, the ponies tossed their heads and snorted. The Hobgoblin Manzukk hurried to greet them. Allie stood beside her adoptive father and brothers, waiting for her grandfather to alight. Willy pulled the door open and lowered the steps. King Finnán Etain had returned to Rois. The Leprechaun king stepped from the coach fussed over by Willy and Manzukk. Allie stepped forward and curtsied to her grandfather and King.

"Alastríona! My child, you are more beautiful than Tiggy and Willy described!" The old king took her in his arms and wept. "It has been far too many years that I have been robbed of my precious family."

A sudden crackling, hissing sound and Dona Angrona appeared in front of them.

"You will be further robbed old man for I remain undefeated!" She shrieked as Kean slammed her to the ground with the sword of the big people at her throat. "You are supposed to be dead!" The witch spluttered, her eyes full of fear and rage. "I sent Ultan to kill you! The Clurichauns lied!" She moaned, the sword burned and blistered her green neck to red.

"I'm very much alive—in fact it's Ultan who is dead, along with most of your Goblins." Kean bared his teeth. "The Clurichauns have surrendered; they no longer answer to you, your curse is failing, they can now tell you any lie they wish."

Maghnus returned with Nyvián and Ronán, scratched and bruised, unhurt but splattered with blood and muck.

"You should kill her now, Kean." Maghnus moved to his side.

"No! Wait!" Allie remembered Orla's words.

Does Orla want Dona Angrona killed?

She prevailed but Kean and the sword of the big people diminished her power, the Goblins had abandoned her.

"I will let you live if you will make reparations to the Clurichauns and Púcas and to all you've damaged. You can serve the rest of your days in prison."

The sorceress' eyes blinked and shifted about, avoiding scrutiny.

"Powerful people like yours murdered my family long ago; they burned them alive, in the name of an all-powerful being they said was loving and merciful. My mother and sisters begged forgiveness—for mercy, but they gave none. I am the last of my kind; they sent me away across the sea." The witch whispered piteously, tears fell from her eyes. "I was a child, alone! They hurt me!" Her strange red eyes widened as she relived the horrors endured through the long, bleak years of her life. "I wanted vengeance! Vengeance in the name of my mother! Don't kill me! Please! I'm not altogether evil!"

Despite losing her family, Allie had known love all of her life and she pitied this hideous witch.

"Don't listen to her, Allie! All she knows is hate and lies!" Kean pressed the sword against the green throat and brought forth another plaintive moan. All around Allie, people shouted, shaking their fists and axes, calling for the witch's head. Angry faces of the Leprechauns and Clurichauns alike, demanding Kean strike her down.

"Allie!" Nyvián took her hand. "Think about what you're doing. This monster is the reason so many have died. She can't be trusted."

Allie trembled; fearful she might do wrong to allow this terrifying sorceress to live, but she hadn't forgotten Orla's words.

Forgiveness is a magic all of its own.

She shouted over the pandemonium, "We are civilised people aren't we? I won't ask my brother or any of you to do cold-blooded murder, and I will not condemn her with death! Not while there is a chance of redemption! I will not drag my people back to the darkness of the past! Jail her! Give her a chance to make amends!" The angry voices grew louder; Allie shouted over them. "Please! Think about what you want for the future of Dorcha Wood. Think about what you want for your families! We can't change the past, but we can change the future!"

Kean studied Allie's face, searching for a sign that his sister may have kissed the blarney stone. He released the witch.

Many things happened at once. Dona Angrona rose to her knees, raised her long green hands, flames erupted and enveloped Allie and Nyvián, billowing bright orange. Her cackling laughter reverberated around the palace forecourt amid the screams of onlookers. The Golden Book in Allie's hand clicked open. High above the palace a deafening bang and a flashing, blinding sphere of lightening, like a tangled ball of string—shrunk, fizzling and hissing to a blinding pinpoint of light—exploded in a shower of sparks followed by a vast ball of red flames and out of the inferno spread a great pair of wings. Orla the Golden Dragon landed in the forecourt and the people scattered. He reared on his hind legs—wings spread wide, his great head lifted skywards and with a mighty roar, he sent a jet of flame high above the Palace of Rois. Tiny hooves drummed as Og charged forward, spun and lashed out with both back feet; he kicked the sorceress in the face, her laughter stopped. Ferghus lunged; his dagger sank into the witch's heart. An iron axe spun through the air and buried in the witch's skull and the silver sword of the big people swished and found its mark. The flames of Dona Angrona's last spell faded and died with her. Tiggy stepped forward, terror and ferocity etched on his kind old face, he retrieved his axe, the blade shattered. Ferghus sprawled, motionless.

"Allie!" Dread shook her brother's voice as he caught her up in his arms.

"I'm unhurt!" Allie struggled to breathe as Kean hugged her. "Her flames didn't touch us, we're not even singed. Orla!"

The Golden Dragon smiled down.

"You did it, Princess Alastríona! Your forgiveness of the sorceress opened the Golden Book and broke the curse I cast on myself. The protection of Dorcha Wood is restored."

Allie studied the book she held. The first page bore an inscription, hand-written in ink. She read it aloud:

'Only the chain of love and friendship, has the power to break the spell. Only the wisdom of people united, by the lessons learned well.'

The following page showed an ink drawing of a man who resembled Kean with the name underneath, *Máedóc Ó hEadhra,* the same man whose statue stood in the town square of Glade Cloch. Allie read the inscription on the opposite page:

'When the sword of the big folk is wielded once more, by the blood of Ó hEadhra; Argent Storm of yore. The life of the Encantar will end but in vain, and the realm of the woodland will prosper again.'

"I don't understand," Kean shook his head. "Who is Máedóc Ó hEadhra?"

"He is your ancestor, Kean O'Hara," Orla's voice rumbled. "A brave and noble warrior."

A motley crowd of furry human-like creatures with big floppy ears and a long tail clopped in, their hard hooves slipping on the stones; they knelt before the King. The Púcas begged his pardon.

Allie took her grandfather's arm. "Please, we must forgive them as well. They're as much victims as are the Clurichauns."

The elderly King smiled at his granddaughter, his old eyes looked into hers.

"This morning I was unwilling to forgive, but today has taught me much. You have wisdom beyond your tender years, Go Púcas, and peace go with you."

Allie saw Fie Fíu and Idé Mae standing together looking lost and sad; she turned to Nyvián and took his hand.

"There is one last thing I have to do and I'll need you to hold my hand—and stand clear if I throw up."

She led Nyvián by the hand, walked to Fie Fíu, and looked into his great teary eyes.

"If you've been telling me a lie I'll find a way to curse you to the end of the earth."

Fie Fíu smiled a watery smile. "Sadly, 'tis one of few truths I've told in the years since I was cursed."

Kean took Allie's side and held hand. His other hand held Aveline's hand and she in turn held the hand of King Liam. A chain formed around the toad and Idé Mae; Orla watched, confused. Allie closed her eyes and held her breath. Compassion warmed her heart as she leaned over and kissed the warty toad on top of his head. As she stepped back a splash of cold water soaked both she and Nyvián from head to toe. Gerry and Mahon stood there holding an empty pail and joined Penny and the rest of the Selkie teens as they roared with laughter. Allie, Nyvián, Kean, and Aveline joined their mirth.

"Oh! Hello, Aunt Madeléine," Nyvián's laughter stopped. Allie looked up to see the Queen of Glade Cloch, a look of outraged astonishment on her pinched face. Her expression softened and Allie saw what she thought might be a trace of a smile.

"Princess!" came a pompous voice from behind her. "How can I ever thank you?"

She turned and there before her stood a portly old Clurichaun, he wore club-toed shoes, a dirty white shirt embroidered in black silk and a ruffled, overtight golden collar. He wore a black silk jacket with puffy sleeves and leggings that may have once been white. A few shabby feathers bedecked the brim of his flat, ornate hat. Sparse grey hair surrounded his mottled, ruddy old face. The curse had lifted from the Clurichauns and once again, there stood before them a leader. Beside him stood a stocky Leprechaun woman, her red hair heavily streaked with silver.

A Clurichaun in the crowd called, "Awl 'ail His Nibs King Florry!"

"'ail! 'ail!" called the other Clurichauns, "'ail! 'ail!"

Patrick O'Hara knelt and hugged Allie. "I'm so proud of you and I know Alastor would be proud too.

33

<u>The Royal Wedding</u>

Plans were underway for a royal wedding and a feast for hundreds of guests. This would be the largest wedding ever witnessed in Dorcha Wood. Guests would come from everywhere—Leprechauns from along the River Síoga, from the mountains to the lands of the Big Folk. The O'Hara family received a special invitation. The Selkies from the Crystal Caves. The Dwarfs of Fuar Lae would bring barrels of their finest ale. The Dragons and the Elves of Orghlaith promised to attend. The Trolls of Tarragon Mountain were invited but it seemed uncertain they'd attend, due to a clash of dates for their triennial gathering of the clans. Troll teen Vraslá would be there for sure, invited to sing her now famous song. The bride and groom loved the age-old dance known as The Midnight Púca-polka and bade the Púcas perform it.

In the village of Kipper Hollow, excitement ran high. They had ordered food, wine, ale, and mead from every available source. This would be an event talked about for years to come. The wedding of King Florry of the Clurichauns to Idé Mae Etain from the Leprechauns, the wedding to seal forever, the bond between the two communities.

A group of excited Clurichaun matrons made Idé Mae's wedding gown, it didn't flatter her but Idé Mae didn't care. Even if made from the woven hair of Hobsnotters, she'd wear it.

Humbled by the compassion and forgiveness shown her by Princess Alastríona, Idé Mae meant never so much as to hurt the feelings of anyone, ever again. She planned to spend every day of the rest of her life helping the sick and the elderly; she would learn medicine from the village midwife and healer, when the old lady passed on, Idé Mae would assume her position. When sickness or injury plagued, it would become a comforting sight to see the chubby little healer bustle in with her basket of medicines. Given her second chance, she would never stop making amends. She hoped that if her father could see her, he would be proud.

Kipper Hollow had no Royal Palace so the wedding took place in the town square. Idé Mae and King Florry wept tears of joy as they said, "I do." They promised to love and care for each other and the folk of Kipper Hollow from that day forward—for rich or for poor—mostly poor—in sickness and in health. The feast and celebrations continued into the early hours, they sang and danced so loud they could hear them across the river in the city of Rois. Nobody complained for all gathered in Kipper Hollow to celebrate with the Clurichauns. King Florry enlisted the help of a few brawny Clurichauns to help him carry his laughing bride, Idé Mae over the threshold and into their humble shack.

Epilogue

Allie checked the wooden box that her father had left her. A silver catch appeared that flipped the lid at her touch. Inside she found a number of keys. One, a tiny silver key which didn't seem to fit anything until her grandfather pointed to the silver crest at the top of the filthy divan. When she touched the key to the crest, it sprang open and a golden ring set with a ruby lay inside.

"Put it on your finger." The ring shrank and moulded itself to fit her middle finger. "Now take the key to the treasury— the large golden key," continued King Finnán. "The treasury won't open without the ring."

Inside sparkled large piles of gold, silver, coins, and precious stones.

"Good thing too." Kean inspected the roughly patched hole in the wall, made by the cannonball. "You're going to need money to repair the damage."

"I'm going to first repair the city." Allie shivered at the light snowflakes drifting in through the gaps and landing on the marble floor, "though on second thought maybe that hole should be fixed before I do anything else."

Allie had never imagined being a Princess could demand so much of her. Restoration of Rois and the Kingdom fell upon her—her grandfather was too infirm for the task. Flannen, Alastor's former guard, had returned to Rois with King Finnán, Allie charged him with keeping order.

"I don't want reprisals brought down on the Clurichauns," she cautioned him, "as long as they're living peaceful law-abiding lives we can ask no more of them."

The Ee-shees, Dragons and the Fae mounted a joint attack on An Dara Choróin and removed the Goblins and their attendant Hobsnotters. Restorations began in preparation for the return of the Clurichauns to their ancestral city.

Manzukk, Tiggy, and Willy took their former positions—Manzukk in charge of the kitchen, Tiggy, the palace butler and Willy, the king's personal valet.

Ferghus made a full recovery and went back to his family in Glade Ceo. He and Maghnus became friends. Maghnus and Madeléine enjoyed one another's company without conflict.

Kean stayed and helped Allie return the city of Rois to its former prosperity. He announced he'd take a trip to Windy Hill Farm to visit his family and would return via Orghlaith. He and Og departed in early autumn. Allie missed him but she had frequent visits from Nyvián to fill the void. She was unwilling to spend any more than a day away from her grandfather, knowing the old man had missed the joy of seeing his only grandchild grow.

The bond between the Big Folk and Little Folk strengthened when a young family moved into Leprechaun's Corner of Windy Hill Farm—a Clurichaun family, and it delighted Patrick O'Hara to have them. He and Mary arrived bearing a pie and two pairs of helping hands to repair Torin's old house.

So there you have it, children, Princess Alastríona broke the curse and freed me, Taliesin the Bard, from the curst Limericks—oh and she turned Fie Fíu back into King Florry. You know—I think I was wrong about Clurichauns, they're really not bad folk at all.

Tis the wee hours and Windy Hill Farm is silent and misty. The wind has stilled and all is quiet. The chirruping of crickets the only sound; and that, children, is the way I like it.

The End

GLOSSARY

<u>**Cast of Characters**</u>

<u>The O'Haras.</u>

Allie (Princess Alastríona Síofra) (Alastríona, pronounced Al-us-tri-ona, is a feminine form of Alastor, second name is pronounced Shiff-ra,).

Patrick and Mary O'Hara – Allie's adoptive parents.

Kean O'Hara – Allie's brother.

Rían O'Hara (pronounced Ryan) – Allie's brother.

Ciara O'Hara – (pronunced Kee-ara) Allie's younger sister.

James O'Hara – Patrick's brother.

Máedóc Ó hEadhra – Ancestor of the O'haras. Ó hEadhra is an ancient form of the name O'Hara.

<u>The Leprechauns.</u>

Torin Etain – cousin to King Finnán Etain.

Idé Mae Etain (pronounced Ida May) – Torin's daughter. (Ide means thirst)

King Angus the Erratic - (Idé Mae's great-grandfather). Deposed.

King Treasach the Truthful. Name means warlike, a fighter. Brother of King Angus.

King Cillian Etain, pronounced Killian – Allie's great-grandfather

King Finnán Etain – Allie's grandfather.

Prince Alastor Etain – Allie's birth father

Lilé – (pronounced Lily) Allie's birth mother.
Flannen – Alastor's captain of the guard.
Tighearnan (Tiggy) – The Kings Butler.
Ullian (pronounced Willian – Irish form of William)
(Willy) The Kings Valet.

The Hobgoblin

Manzukk – From Fuar Lae, longtime resident of Rois, a
devoted and much loved servant of King Finnán.

The Clurichauns

Fie Fíu – (The second part of his name means wart.)
Pronounced Fee -foo.
Ultan – Ultan the Evil

The Grants

Og the Defender. Og means small.
Ki the Courageous (a female grant)

The Fae

Eaghan – King – Maghnus and Madeléine's father.
Isabelle – Allies great grandmother. Married to
Prince/King Cillian of Rois
Maghnus (pronounced Magnus) Nyvián's father.
Ríona (Maghnus' wife) means queenly.
Madeléine (pronounced Madeleen) – Queen of Glade
Cloch.
Nyvián –   Faerie Prince and heir to the throne of Glade
Cloch.
Moyna – the Faerie Queen's maidservant and companion

Anrie – (Pronounced "On-ray" Irish form of Henry.) The
Queen's head butler.
Aenghus – a guard at Glade Ceo.
Ferghus – The cursed Faerie.

<u>The Residents of Orghlaith and Tarragon Mountain.</u>
Orla – the ancient golden dragon that was a former ally
and resident of Rois.
Aveline – Princess and grand-daughter of King Liam
Seamus, Niall, Garbhan, Lorcan. Elven soldiers.
Luisech (pronounced Lucy) – soldier and the only other
girl in Aveline's company.
Liam – Elven King
Liadan – Elven Queen – means grey lady.
Prince Sarrián – Son of Liam and Liadan. Aveline's father.
Gilroy – Orla's butler - Means son of the king's servant.
Captain Glearán.
Ragnel – a leader of the Trolls.
Vraslá – female teenage troll and guide.
Alegutt Anvilarm - the dwarf and blacksmith. Resides in
Orghlaith. Hails from the Mountains of Fuar Lae.

<u>The Shape-shifter/witch/Sorceress/Encantar.</u> (These are all the
same person)
Dona Angrona – witch.
Creven – means fox.
Ivor – King Eaghan's Viceroy

<u>Selkies.</u>
Tadg – leader of the Selkies.

283

Ronán – Tadg's son and Selkie warrior.
Lonán, Odrán, Ladg, Hadrán and Malag – Selkie warriors.
Penny (F) Neasa (F) Gerry (M) Mahon (M) – Selkie teens.
Dugán – The Selkie's medicine man.

The Goblins
    Captain Zuunk Mosskull
    Gnosag

The Hobsnotters – Rat sized people that live in Dorcha Wood.

Púcas – Shapeshifting Goblin Faeries.

The Ee-shees – Guardians of the woods, mainly they protect the trees.

Taliesin The Bard – The singer, storyteller and prophet of Dorcha Wood.

Place Names and their meanings.

    Windy Hill Farm- Ah begorrah! 'tis windy!
    Fuar Lae – Cold day. (Foo-er – lay) means cold.
    Rois – Means King - also means rose.
    Aois (lake near Rois) means "Old".
    Breagha – (Means Lovely) County Breagha and Breagha Village.

Dorcha Wood – Dorcha means dark

Turloug – Dry lake – (Along with Rois is the ancestral home of the Leprechauns)

Caonach – Moss

Glade Ceo (kee-oh) – Ceo means mist or fog.

Glade Cloch – Cloch means stone.

An Dara Choróin – means second crown.

Kipper Hollow (Along with An Dara Choróin – is the ancestral home of the Clurichauns)

Tarragon Mountain – Ancestral home of the Elves and Trolls. Tarragon means dragon.

Orghlaith – Means golden. (the city where Orla dwells)

Síoga River – Síoga means Faerie.

Fada Wood (Fada means far)

Daione's Path – People's path (Pronounced Dee-nee)

The Crystal Caves – ancestral home of the Selkies.

Púca Flats – the ancestral home of the Púcas.

Other notes.

Cittern – An Irish stringed instrument with 10 strings in sets of 2 to play as 5 strings.

The Bluebell is a symbol of freedom.

The Daisy is a symbol of Innocence and Gentleness.

The Rose is a symbol of love, honour and wisdom.

Ériu – The Goddess of Ireland.

BIOGRAPHY

A. Isobel Sutcliffe lives in Western Queensland, Australia with her husband, two dogs and two cats. She has an adult son and daughter. A child of grazier parents, she grew up in remote rural Queensland. She spent thirty-three years as a working musician. A visual artist she turned to writing in 2015.

For any of Ms. Sutcliffe's other works, please visit JaCol publishing at www.jacolpublishing.com